Enough is Enough

THOMAS WAUGH

© Thomas Waugh 2019

Thomas Waugh has asserted his rights under the Copyright, Design and Patents Act, 1988, to be identified as the author of this work.

First published in 2019 by Sharpe Books.

CONTENTS

Chapters 1 – 22

Epilogue

End Note

ENOUGH IS ENOUGH

> *"Aren't we all better dead?"*
> Graham Greene, *The Quiet American.*

> *"I'm fed up with all these untidy, casual affairs that leave me with a bad conscience."*
> Ian Fleming, *On Her Majesty's Secret Service.*

1.

Music played in the background. Dylan, again.

"Ain't it just like the night to play tricks when you're tryin' to be so quiet?

We sit here stranded though we're all doing our best to deny it..."

James Marshal peered out his living room window again and balled his hand into a fist. The ex-soldier's square jaw grew even squarer as he compressed his teeth together. The easy half-smile, which he usually wore in public and in private, fell from his face, like shit sliding off a shovel.

The pair were there again, sitting in their car, parked at the end of his street. Wearing too much jewellery. Covered in too many tattoos. Scaring too many people, inside their own homes. Selling too many drugs.

Enough is enough.

There was a police station around the corner, but it may as well have been a hundred miles away. The police were probably too busy investigating the latest hate crime on Twitter, or building a case against a deceased celebrity, to address what was happening under their nose. It would have been funny, if it wasn't true. Or perhaps it was funny, because it was true, Marshal wryly considered.

They were, most likely, Albanians. He had read the odd article recently about how they had taken control of drugs and prostitution in Glasgow. And now they were looking to expand their activities in London. There was an ongoing turf war in Walworth and Camberwell. The Albanians versus the West Indians. Petty crime was up. Drug-related deaths were up. Stabbings and shootings were up. Human trafficking was up. Everything was up, Marshal judged, including stealth taxes and his cholesterol levels.

This was the third time, in a week, that the two men had sat at the end of his street. Every now and then a customer would approach the car and a wad of notes would be exchanged for a bag of weed or coke. Customers ranged from tracksuit wearing skanks to city workers in designer suits. The Albanians reminded Marshal of the Taliban, back in Helmand. They were akin to vermin. Once they established a foothold in an area, it was almost impossible to get rid of them. But, like vermin, they needed to be exterminated. Despite not always winning the battles – and losing the war – Marshal had felt purposeful as a soldier. Killing the enemy – and protecting his fellow soldiers – felt good. Right. Perhaps if he was able to make a difference here, it would serve as a penance for the defeat over there. Bombings in Kabul, the closing down of schools and the executions of homosexuals were all up over there. The former 3 Para Captain still experienced a bitter taste in his mouth when he thought about the war in Afghanistan – as much as he had tried to wash the taste away with copious amounts of vodka and whisky over the years.

He breathed out, or rather sighed. Marshal was forty. Life was supposed to begin at forty, or so the saying went. His face was still handsome, but looked lived-in. Life had chipped away at his smooth, marble features. Afghanistan, or London, had aged him. Ground him down. His eyes were a little bloodshot. His bark-brown hair was dusted with a little grey.

"...Name me someone that's not a parasite and I'll go out and say a prayer for him..."

Marshal was wearing a navy-blue linen suit, striped white shirt and brown Oxford brogues. He looked better than he felt. He was about to head out, to have dinner with Alison, a book editor he had met at a party a fortnight ago. This would be their third date. He had slept with her on the second. It was likely this would be their last date though, Marshal judged. He didn't feel much, if anything, for her. They had no real future together. It was best to end things now. *Be cruel to be kind.* What was the point of lying to her, or himself? There was enough deceit in the world, without him adding to the surplus. Marshal wanted to have a nice meal with Alison this evening, and he hoped they might even have sex again, if she took the break-up well.

The news was playing on the TV, but the sound was mute. Marshal didn't care for inane or partisan commentators, filling his flat with lies or orthodoxy. Rather he just liked to read the straplines along the bottom of the screen, informing him about the bare bones of events. Not that he cared much about most events, or "human interest" stories. *"Nothing exists except atoms and empty space; everything else is opinion,"* Marshal often thought to himself, quoting Democritus. If only people could laugh at themselves more – or shrug their shoulders at the causes they cared about. Or told people they cared about. The world might then be a more pleasant place.

If Marshal was able to sleep with Alison tonight, he thought it best to do so at her apartment. He needed to clean his. Vesuvius-shaped mounds of ash and cigarette butts filled a couple of large ashtrays in the room. A half-empty bottle of vodka lay on the floor, next to an empty tumbler. A plate, caked with takeaway curry from the night before, sat on the coffee table, next to a curled-up copy of *Gun Monthly*.

A bookcase, brimming with Penguin Classics (Tolstoy, Balzac, Dostoyevsky, Graham Greene...) stood next to one overladen with military history titles. On the opposite side of the room stood further bookcases, one dedicated to medieval history and the other to the ancient world. His bedroom housed a series of bookshelves devoted to crime/thrillers, poetry and philosophy books. Contemporary novels and non-fiction titles concerning events of the last fifty years were conspicuous by their absence. Along with several bookcases, the room was also home to a few pieces of oak and mahogany furniture (some were antique, some were just old). A series of character jugs (of Henry V, Wellington, General Wolfe and Churchill) sat in the same display case as a series of plates depicting the story of *Operation Chastise* – the Dambusters Raid. Further objects of militaria, dotted throughout the room, could be found in the shape of a pair of nineteenth-century duelling pistols, a replica medieval sword and a Winchester rifle, mounted on the wall. The musty smell hanging in the air gave the room a further sense that the house could have belonged to a fusty Professor or retired Major – or, if one observed the portrait of Nelson and an antique naval telescope, a retired Admiral.

Marshal took another long drag on his cigarette and turned his attention to the night sky, rather than the street below. The horizon glowed like embers, or the flesh of a peach. The light was fading. He was reminded of his time as an altar boy, as he doused out the torch candles, plunging the church into darkness. There was light in the darkness, however, in the form of the votive candles. His mother always gave him money, to put into the box, light one and say a prayer. She was a good, devoted, Catholic. Unfortunately, he couldn't say the same about himself. His mother had died when he was young. When she was young. Too young. Marshal still kept her Bible in the drawer, although he couldn't recall the last time he opened it. He was just six years old when she died. Mary Marshal often counselled her son, that "love can conquer all." Unfortunately, it couldn't seem to cure her cancer. He remembered her taking him to church and teaching him to swim. He remembered how she looked as pale as candlewax in the hospital, at the end. It hurt her throat each time she spoke, but still, she told her son how much she loved him. Marshal also remembered how angry he was at God for taking her away. The world was a worse place without her. Perhaps he was still angry at God for taking her too soon. At best God was indifferent. Why shouldn't he be indifferent to God in return?

Marshal glared down at the street again. Unforgiving and unimpressed. Despite the descending gloom, the eagle-eyed soldier could still see the Albanians clearly. His blood was simmering. It would soon boil over. It wasn't that Marshal couldn't control his temper. Far from it. In the heat of battle in Helmand, the officer kept a cool head. His heartbeat quickened, but never accelerated out of control. Any adrenaline rush he experienced never caused him to snatch at a shot or issue the wrong order, as to fight or flight. Marshal owned more confirmed kills than any other officer in the regiment – and God only knows how many unconfirmed kills he secured. He believed that violence could be a force for good, that the world was a better place for him having removed a number of Taliban from it.

He glanced at his watch and yawned. He had stayed up late the previous evening. Marshal could often be found awake in the dead of night, reading. He had woken-up late and taken a walk around Kennington Park in the morning. He was tempted to go swimming, but the pool would have been busy. Marshal may not have agreed with Sartre's communist sympathies. But he agreed with the writer's sentiment, that "hell is other people." Marshal found a quiet corner of a pub and had lunch and a few pints after his walk. His army pension, and a significant inheritance from his grandfather, meant that Marshal had no need to work. He lived comfortably. Even contentedly. He returned home to answer several emails and arrange his online food order for the week. He also ordered a first edition copy of *The First Crusade* by Runciman, before taking a nap. When he stirred, he downed a large whisky. It was whilst looking out the window, checking to see if it would rain, when Marshal spotted the car.

Enough was enough.

Marshal stubbed out his cigarette, picked up his keys and turned the music and television off.

Drug dealers. They thought themselves an immovable object. But they were about to encounter an unstoppable force.

2.

Marshal noticed a slight chill in the air, in contrast to the balmy temperature earlier in the day. The weather, like a woman, couldn't make up its mind. He exited his block. He could have still turned left, instead of right, and avoided the car. But his course was, Ahab-like, set.

Marshal's large tenement building ran down one side of the street. The Victorian brick building, part of the *Pullens Estate*, was old – which was part of the reason why Marshal had chosen to live there. Terracotta arches over the doorways and dozens of flowering window boxes increased the attractiveness of the block. The neighbourhood was a nice one, because of and not in spite of the fact that young professionals didn't quite outnumber the working-class locals. At the opposite end of the street, to the Albanians, stood a primary school. *Crampton*. Apparently, Charlie Drake had attended the school. Aside from during the school-run, the street was relatively quiet, which was perhaps why the drug dealers chose to park there. A few streetlamps bathed part of the scene in a soft, amber glow.

His mind and body snapped to attention, like heels on a parade ground, as he took in the scene, noting any escape routes and weapons to hand. Thankfully, the Albanians didn't notice him come out of his doorway. A small-set, rat-faced figure sat in the driver's seat. Vasil Bisha. His spiked, black hair was full of product – and appeared as oily as a Cabinet minister. His skin was pale, waxy. His features were shaped into a perpetual sneer, as if he were just about to spit out a gobbet of phlegm. His teeth, housed within swollen gums, were sharp and yellow, like shards of antique ivory. Beady eyes sat beneath a beetle brow. There was something inherently feral and nasty about the man, Marshal considered. He probably carried a knife and wouldn't think twice about stabbing someone in the back. Bisha had worked as a hospital porter, back in Tirana, before his cousin encouraged him to come to Britain, over a decade ago.

"It is a land of milk and money, Vasil," his kinsman argued. "You can earn more in a month in Britain than you can in a year in the old country... Luka Rugova, our boss, will treat you well... Besa, our code, is everything. Always obey any order. Your loyalty will be to Luka... Do not think about crossing Baruti, Luka's lieutenant, either. He's as cunning as a fox and as vicious as a mongoose... We're a family..."

Vasil Bisha worked his way up in the organisation. He had been specially recruited by Rugova to come down to London, from Glasgow, and build up their businesses. He sold product. He drove prostitutes to outcall clients. He collected money each week from their brothels, or money laundering units. Business was good. Life was good. Bisha was fond of sampling his own product a little too much, however, as evidenced by his constant sniffing and erratic moods. He also enjoyed sampling the new girls he helped traffic over. He liked them young, before they turned into sour-faced hags. He would sometimes give a tip to the ones he liked, but should he be unhappy with their performance or lack of respect for him, Bisha would get rough with them. On one occasion, when he broke a girl's cheekbone, Rugova had to warn his employee about his conduct. The girl couldn't work for several weeks – and Bisha was ordered to pay compensation to the brothel, out of his wages, for the organisation's loss of earnings. Business was business.

The figure in the passenger seat, Bashkim, resembled a Slavic Frankenstein's monster, Marshal thought. Brutal and gormless. Bullet-headed. Lantern-jawed. The former boxer had cauliflower ears and a flat, broken nose, resembling a statue whose beak had been clumsily re-attached. His drug of choice seemed to be body-building steroids, rather than cocaine. Bashkim's neck was decorated with a large tattoo of the double-headed eagle, featured on the Albanian flag. He wore tracksuit bottoms and a body-hugging t-shirt, revealing a tattoo of a knife, dripping with blood, on one forearm, and an image of a black bear on the other. Spiderweb tattoos covered his knuckles and the webbing on his hands, which contained several gold rings. Bashkim wore a diamond earring on his left ear and a thick, gold chain around his neck. Marshal sensed that the thug possessed more money than sense, though he couldn't be blamed for being alone in the world in that regard. You had to spend a significant amount of money to buy something so ugly.

Bashkim had joined Rugova's gang after finishing his national service. From the start, he proved an enthusiastic, effective enforcer. He embraced the Besa code. He nicknamed himself "The Butcher," because he wasn't afraid of getting blood on his hands and because the foot-soldier came from a family of fishmongers and butchers, back in his hometown of Klos. Bashkim had recently become Rugova's chief torturer, although Baruti invariably oversaw any interrogation. "The Butcher" took pride in his work – and enjoyed watching his victims writhe in agony and scream, almost operatically. His favourite method of torture was just to take out his cigarette lighter and use the flame to burn noses, eyes and genitals. Bashkim would often extend the session of torture, even when Baruti had extracted the relevant information from his victim. The Albanian enjoyed mixing business with pleasure.

Bashkim had also recently become obsessed with posting semi-naked pictures and videos of himself on Facebook. He would oil up his skin and flex his muscles, sometimes holding a knife and licking the blade. He even generated quite a few followers, in the form of Albanian criminals/prisoners, housewives from Peterborough and gay men. He constantly checked whether his pictures were being "liked" and commented on. There were times when Bashkim wanted to boast of his crimes on his page, but he knew Baruti would frown on him doing so. Things must be kept within the family.

Bishka turned down the rap music that was playing as the potential customer came up to his car door. Thank God for small mercies, Marshal thought. The wiry Albanian was smoking a cigarette, with the window down.

"What are you looking for?" the dealer asked, before sniffing and stroking his thumb across his nose. His accent was guttural, but his English was good. The phrase he used was not altogether incriminating. The dealer had sent a text message to a raft of regular customers to say where he was, but he was all too willing to sell to new people as well.

"I'm looking for you to drive away and ply your wares elsewhere," Marshal replied, politely yet firmly. "Nothing good can come of you staying here." Although the Hampshire-born soldier had attended Harrow, Magdalen and Sandhurst, his voice had acquired a slight London drawl over the years. The onetime captain in 3 Para had been as comfortable drinking in the barracks as in the officer's mess.

Bishka's weaselly features creased in confusion and contempt. For a moment, he thought that the stranger might be drunk, or an undercover policeman. But it seemed he was just a nosey neighbour. The English thought they were so superior – although, having lived in Glasgow for a few years, he considered that the English had reason to believe themselves superior to the Scottish.

"Who the fuck are you?" Bishka said, or snarled, baring his sharp yellow teeth. His Balkan accent grew more pronounced, as his irritation increased. His native tongue was lodged in his throat, as firmly as an arrow had pierced Harold Godwinson's eye. You can take the boy out of Albania, but you cannot take Albania out of the boy. Although Marshal judged that was slightly unfair. He had known more than one decent Albanian who had settled in England and flourished. Darden, the owner of a café near his grandfather's house in Eltham. He was a sweet, hardworking man, devoted to his family. And then there was Mira, a half-Albanian insurance broker he had dated many moons ago. She could be vocal in and out bed. If only, like his remote control, Mira had come with a mute button.

"I would say that I am a concerned citizen, but I'm much more of a staunch royalist – and therefore a subject instead of a citizen. Too few people nowadays seem to have any genuine devotion to our Queen and country, unfortunately," the former officer stated, his tone still equitable. He still held out a slither of hope that the Albanians would drive off. That trouble could be avoided. Yet man is born to trouble as surely as sparks fly upward.

Bashkim muttered something to his confederate in what Marshal imagined to be Albanian. If he had said something in Latin or Medieval French then Marshal might have recognised the words, from his time at Oxford. Bisha nodded in reply and took another drag on his cigarette. Marshal noticed his nicotine-stained fingers and a small swastika tattoo behind his ear. Both subtle and unsubtle.

"You reckon yourself to be some sort of good Samaritan? I can tell you, God will not protect you should we have to get out of this car and teach you some manners."

"Good Samaritan? No. I'm Old Testament rather than New, if anything. I certainly believe God should be more vengeful than merciful."

Enough was enough, for Bisha. He was proving a nuisance. The drug dealer also didn't want the stranger to scare off any genuine customers. He just needed to tell Bashkim to get out of the car. The arrogant Englishman's balls would retreat up inside him and he would scurry away. As an initial act of intimidation and spite, however, Bisha flicked his cigarette at the irritant.

Before the butt had time to bounce off his chest and hit the ground Marshal reached out and grabbed the small Albanian. Shock and awe. He pulled Bisha through the car window, in a matter of seconds, and then threw him onto the road, as if he were a ragdoll. Bisha first yelped and then groaned, winded. *Once they're down, make sure they stay down.* Marshal knew he needed to take the first man out of the fight, before the second one entered the fray. He quickly stamped on Bisha's groin and then stamped on his head, twice, knocking the Albanian unconscious.

Bashkim let out a curse, retrieved a knife from the glovebox and scrambled out of the car. As well as acting as an enforcer, his principal duty was to protect his comrade.

"You need to look after Bisha, even more than you need to look after yourself," Baruti had drummed into him, like needles repeatedly jabbing his skin to produce a tattoo. "Why?"

"Because he carries the money," Bashkim had repeatedly, dutifully, answered.

In letting Bisha come to harm he had tarnished his honour, trust. Besa. He would redeem himself by punishing the Englishman. He would not kill him, as Baruti needed to sanction such an action. Murder attracted too much attention and was potentially bad for business. But he would make him bleed. Hurt him. Perhaps he would slice open a hamstring or cut off an ear.

Bashkim walked, or waddled, around the front of the car like a sumo wrestler. He was 6'3". As powerful – and lumbering – as an ox. His chest jutted out like the prow of a tugboat. The meat cleaver was spotted with bloodstains. Marshal retreated a little. The hulking Albanian grinned at his prey, his gold teeth shining like the oversized, vulgar chain around his thick, shock-absorbing neck. He felt like a wolf, who had cornered a sheep. Bashkim wondered if the stranger was part of a rival gang. If so though, which one? Surely the West Indians wouldn't employ a white man? Although, because it was so unexpected, perhaps they were responsible for the attack.

Marshal retreated even more, walking backwards towards the other side of the street. His features grew taut, like a finger tightening around the trigger of a gun. The Albanian was tough. But not tough, or smart, enough. Marshal reached the kerb and picked up the half-brick he had spotted earlier, as he approached the car. He needed to make his throw count. If he aimed too low the missile might glance off his opponent, like a tin can pinging off a wall. If he aimed too high the Albanian might be able to duck and avoid the blow.

A grimace replaced the grin on Bashkim's face. The red brick loomed large in the Englishman's hands. He was ready and willing to use it. The Albanian hesitated, caught between charging at his opponent or retreating. Marshal hesitated not. The former Harrovian wicket keeper launched the brick, with speed and accuracy, as if it were a cricket ball. It struck his enemy on the chin. A blurriness, rather than blackness, afflicted the enforcer's sight. He swayed, like a drunk in a dockside pub. Blood dribbled down his chin, like spittle from a baby's mouth. Bashkim was momentarily disorientated. But a moment was all Marshal needed. He ran forward and buried his foot into the big man's groin, as if he were kicking to convert a try. The excruciating pain shot through him like a lightning bolt, sprouting up from the road. He slumped to the ground, the cleaver falling from out of his hand, further disorientated. Defeated. *Once they're down, make sure they stay down.* Marshal – his face a paradigm of impassiveness – crunched his heel down on his fingers, as if squashing a cockroach. Blood seeped from his already scarred knuckles. A couple of the bones cracked. In order to immobilise his opponent – and ensure he wasn't followed – Marshal jumped-up and thrust his foot down at the same time in order to shatter the Albanian's ankle. The enforcer seethed rather than howled in agony. His entire body seemed to throb with pain. He didn't quite know which part of him hurt the most. The ex-boxer was down for the count.

Bashkim muttered another curse, or perhaps he asked who the stranger was, but the Englishman was already out of earshot. He walked over to the still unconscious Bisha, reached into his pockets and stole his wallet and phone. Marshal sensed this might be the start, as opposed to end, of something.

Know your enemy.

3.

The night was a giant mouth, attempting to swallow up all the people. The gadflies. The lights – from the cars, buildings and streetlamps – were the monster's teeth. The jaws never quite clamped down on all the vapid lovers and imbeciles, shouting into their phones, who populated the scene, Marshal considered. People piled onto buses, without letting the passengers off first, like a clamour to get through the gates of heaven or hell. One youth elbowed an elderly lady in the face. The sickly smell of weed hung in the air, like a faded gravy stain stuck on a lapel. Every other person jabbed their fingers against their phones, sending off vacuous or vicious tweets. London resembled a cesspool, rather than Plato's Republic, Marshal judged, recalling Cicero's quote about Rome.

Marshal still felt a tingle in his foot from where it had inflicted so much damage. He was keen for his foot to also connect with the next cyclist who ran a red light. His fists almost felt jealous or deficient, from not being able to pull their weight. By the time he reached the end of Walworth Road, Marshal's heartbeat had returned to its normal, nonchalant cadence. He was uninjured, unlike his opponents. It had been a good fight. They had started the contest, from a certain point of view. He had ended it. They could now retreat and lick their wounds. *God knows what will happen next.* The battle was over, but that did not mean that the war was. Any victory is only temporary, albeit defeats always feel more permanent. It couldn't do any harm to gather more intelligence on his enemy. He was reminded of a phrase his mother used to say to him: "It doesn't do any harm to pray". But Marshal wanted to shunt the gargoyle images of the Albanians from his mind's eye.

It was only polite that he turned his attention towards Alison. They had met around a fortnight ago, at a bar in Blackfriars. She was having a drink with some friends, after work. Marshal was sat reading in the corner, keeping himself to himself. She approached and asked if she could take the empty chair by his table. She then enquired as to what he was reading. She was curious, for professional reasons – as she worked as a commissioning editor for a mainstream publisher. They started talking and Marshal bought Alison a drink, and another one. He liked her. She wasn't taken back, too much, by his black and dry humour. She could carry off a cocktail dress and walk effortlessly in heels, after a bottle of wine. They exchanged numbers. An unremarkable first date nevertheless turned into a second. Sex at the end of the second date put a favourable gloss on the evening. Lust has the ability to paper over the cracks when there's a lack of true affection. But the more Marshal got to know Alison, the less he liked her. He initially thought Alison would be well-read, and they could talk about literature and history. But the only classics she had read were those on her academic course list. She also preferred to listen to podcasts nowadays, as opposed to reading for pleasure. The fiction editor hadn't even heard of Turgenev, let alone read one of his novels. Marshal thought to himself how he could never marry anyone who hadn't read the Russian. The daughter of a Guardian journalist was rude to waiters – and ruder still to pretty waitresses. She took pictures of her meals and posted them on Instagram. She also spent ten minutes bemoaning Brexit because she might have to replace her Polish cleaner and pay more as a result. He couldn't quite work out Alison's chief sin. Was it that she was unintelligent or tedious?

Small things add up.

Modern women are second only to modern men for being shallow and self-serving, Marshal lamented. In a spirit of equality – and he was unsure whether this made him a feminist or not – he considered that women were just as susceptible to conceit and cruelty as men. Women were perhaps guiltier of the curse of the age: virtue-signalling. Although some feminists might have argued that the curse of the age was climate change, or cultural appropriation, or patriarchal society. Or actors being paid more than actresses. Or a lack of safe-spaces in universities.

Marshal's thoughts wandered on to previous women he had hurt, rather than been hurt by. He was more sinning than sinned against, he realised. They paraded through his mind like a procession of the dead.

Tanya. He had dated her just after he became an officer. She was sweet, fun. His father, Donald, didn't approve that she was a hairdresser and the daughter of a lowly window cleaner. Marshal didn't approve, however, when he found out Tanya had stopped taking the pill. She wanted to trap him, be a soldier's wife. He didn't desire to be a husband or a father. Especially the latter. Who would want to bring a child into such a dire world? A world where Bono existed. "I want you to make an honest woman of me," Tanya had argued. Marshal countered that she would be unable to make an honest man of him, if such a thing existed – and confessed how he had cheated on her with one of her closest friends.

Petra. Cambridge graduate. Law conversion. Petra lived in Wandsworth, but constantly spoke about her dream to live in Richmond. She had partly dated the soldier because she knew her father, a fundraiser for the Green Party, would disapprove. For some reason, the spark went out of their relationship when he found out she was an evangelical atheist and member of the National Secular Society. Not that Marshal was a devout Christian. Or devout anything. But when she declared that Catholicism was evil, he could never envision marrying her. Or loving her.

Rebecca. A Home Office civil servant. Devoted to her job. She seemed to love the Conservative government more than him. Although Marshal was capable of a healthy amount of self-loathing, he rightly didn't consider himself more loathsome than a number of Tory politicians. She was clinical in her love-making, as if it were a box-ticking exercise on an official government document. Her cut-glass vowels suddenly became too shrill for him one day. He would wince, as if he could hear the sound of fingernails scraping down a blackboard, every time Rebecca opened her mouth. Marshal also distrusted anyone who was more overtly right-wing than he was.

Caroline. An airhostess. Due to her work, they barely saw one another, which was probably the reason why their relationship lasted for so long. The sex was great, but conversation stilted. She talked and he half-listened. They eventually asked themselves what they had in common, aside from agreeing on how good the sex was. The answer was nothing. Nothing can come of nothing.

A handful of the women in Marshal's life had remarked that they loved him, over the years. Most had uttered the words after sex – or after drinking several glasses of wine. Some had done so because they judged he wanted to hear it, or they wanted to hear him say it back. But Marshal could never bring himself to reciprocate. To lie. He hoped that his silence said enough.

Mayflies have longer and more meaningful relationships, Marshal wryly thought as he arrived at Waterloo. He saw that Chekhov's *Ivanov* was playing at the Old Vic theatre and made a mental note to book tickets and take someone. It just wouldn't be Alison.

The restaurant was situated beneath some railway arches. Perhaps someone thought that the neon glass and aluminium décor would fit well with the old brick walls and brass fittings. They were wrong. The lighting was too harsh, the volume of the Euro-trash music even harsher. The cuisine was French-British. It seemed to Marshal to just be an excuse to douse every dish in butter and jus, served with a portion of triple-cooked chips. He would have preferred to have his chips cooked once and to pay a third of the price for them.

Marshal saw Alison sitting in the far corner. She was on her phone, doubtless chatting to people on her WhatsApp group. He apologised for being a little late, feeling genuinely guilty for his tardiness. Alison was wearing a red, wraparound sleeveless dress, which showed off both her figure and holiday tan. A recently trimmed bob framed a soft, round, pretty face. Her jade eyes widened and gleamed, competing with the candlelight on the table, when she saw Marshal. She smiled, effusively, like a bride. Alison had just sent a text message to a friend to say that the wealthy, ex-officer could be "the one". As much courage as he displayed confronting the Albanians, Marshal realised he did not have it in him to break-up with the woman over dinner. He would do so afterwards, in a more cowardly fashion. He didn't want a scene – or to see her hurt.

"How was your day?" he asked, once he had settled down and ordered a bottle of wine. He only drank wine by the bottle, as opposed to the glass.

Alison rolled her eyes, sighed and vented. Marshal noted how she failed to thank the waitress for pouring out her glass of wine.

"It was a pain! We had an acquisitions meeting, with the sales team. God, they're as moronic as anyone who voted for Brexit. They turned down the book I have been working on for the past two months. The agent and I sweated blood and tears getting the novel into shape. They said the author, who has been on the panel of Loose Women for Christ's sake, didn't have a sufficient amount of Twitter followers. She isn't marketable, which is code for saying she is too old."

Marshal made a face to express sympathy. He didn't really understand Twitter and couldn't care less if a minor, or major, celebrity had written a book.

"How was your day?" Alison finally asked, after telling him about the new Mulberry handbag and Michael Kors watch she had bought, to cheer herself up.

"As dull as dishwater, I'm afraid. You're comfortably the highlight of my evening," he replied, charmingly.

"How's your food?" Alison asked, hoping that Marshal was enjoying his meal, as she had read a review on a food blog and picked the eatery.

"Delicious," he replied, lying. His sea bass was smothered in too much butter and garlic. His chips were cold, and the wine wasn't cold enough. But he ploughed through the meal and bottle. Perhaps the fight had helped him work-up an appetite. Marshal bit his tongue on more than one occasion, as Alison gripped her phone and responded to numerous messages throughout dinner. She often said "sorry" whilst doing so, but with scant sincerity. Few people are genuinely contrite nowadays. We don't answer to God, so why should we answer to our fellow man?

Marshal was guilty of being distracted throughout the evening too. He was monosyllabic in his answers, detached, when she probed him for his opinions on what was happening in the world, or on reality TV. There was so much that Marshal didn't care about. It was almost awe-inspiring. He considered so many heartfelt views, or ideological convictions, comical. Or tragic. Or comical for being tragic. Marshal believed in irony, that there were two sides to a story. And both sides were equally wrong, as well as tedious.

All is vanity under the sun.

He drank heavily, reaching for his glass like a nervous tic. He tapped his foot beneath the table, yearning to leave and/or craving a cigarette. When Alison left to visit the toilet, Marshal yawned so much he feared he may dislocate his jaw. He forced the odd polite smile, pulling his own strings, like a puppeteer, to please his audience. As much as Alison was a picture of health and attractiveness in front of him, Marshal's mind's eye focussed on the image of the two Albanians leaving the scene. They would either visit their boss or the hospital. But would they be ordered to pay a visit to Marshal at a later date?

After dessert, with Marshal seemingly relaxed with a large brandy in front of him, Alison decided to ask about his time in the army again. She told herself she was being considerate, that she wanted to get to know him more. If he was still scarred by his time in Afghanistan, she wanted to help heal his pain. But Marshal liked to keep his pain to himself, like a leprechaun hiding his treasure.

"Being a soldier mostly means waiting around. Waiting in line to eat. Waiting to sleep. Waiting for meetings which get cancelled at the last minute. Waiting to go on patrol. Waiting to come back from patrol... The enemy is often boredom... People think soldiers come back from war laden with nightmares or war stories. Most Paras I know came back from the war laden with the pox, however, from stopping off in Berlin or Prague... I wish I had more to tell you," Marshal explained, shrugging his shoulders in conclusion whilst thinking about paying the bill.

In truth, there was plenty more that the ex-soldier could have spoken about, in relation to the war and his former profession. He could have mentioned the waiting – for the enemy mortars to start and mortars to stop. How the army had the stomach for the fight, but their politicians didn't. Special advisers and focus groups acted as their commander-in-chief. Helicopters were promised, but Santa and his reindeer had more chance of arriving at the base. Lions led by donkeys. Or asses. Part of Marshal's duties involved babysitting government officials. More often than not they would shit themselves, and not from having eaten the local cuisine, when they heard shots fired in anger. He remembered one oleaginous minister proclaiming, at a press conference, that the people of Afghanistan were the "friendliest people in the world". If true, Marshal would have hated to meet the unfriendliest people in the world. Or they were "good people". Good people, who grew poppies, harboured the Taliban, gave intelligence to their enemies, planted IEDs, subjugated women and executed homosexuals.

Marshal imagined how Alison wanted to ask the same question which remained on the tips of the tongues of others. Had he killed anyone? But she wouldn't like the answer. And she wouldn't like to hear how Marshal hadn't lost any sleep about shooting his fellow human beings. Fellow human beings, who wanted to shoot him too. Killing became second nature to the Para. Or perhaps it was something even more primal than second nature. Soldiering was in his blood. Both his father and grandfather had served in the army. Killing might have been in his blood too. Whilst in Helmand, Marshal wanted to murder a hundred Taliban to avenge any death on his side. And he considered that a charitable rate of exchange.

Alison asked, when they were in bed before, if the wound, from where he was shot in the shoulder, still hurt. It did. But Marshal said it didn't. He didn't want her pity. He just wanted her body, to temporarily take the pain away.

THOMAS WAUGH

4.

The temperature dropped as Marshal left the restaurant. The firmament was cloudless yet also seemingly starless. A blanket of pollution, or folly, smothered the sky. But even if it was fretted with majesty and glimmering constellations, he fancied that most people would still have their heads buried in their phones. It was sometimes worth venturing out into the countryside, just to see the stars.

Alison was slightly taken back when Marshal mentioned he was tired and couldn't come back to her place. Her features suddenly became delicate, downturned – as if she were a child who had displeased her parents, but she didn't quite know why. They parted company after he kissed her on the cheek. Alison's rueful expression turned to one of rage, however, after he sent his text. London used to lubricate itself on gin, nourished by a sense of humour. Now anger and grievance were written into most souls, like lettering running through a stick of rock. People rush to take offence, as if receiving some form of benediction for doing so. Marshal thought he had been reasonable in his message. He argued that he was not ready for a serious relationship, that he couldn't give Alison what she wanted. *It's me, not you.*

"You're a bastard," Alison included in one of her messages. Tears would dampen her pillow later in the night.

"I know. I'm sorry," Marshal typed back. Any awkwardness he felt was tempered by the feeling that he was glad it was all over. He tried to be honest, but he knew from experience that most women preferred dishonesty. He put in his earphones and walked on, drowning out the sounds of blaring sirens and bleating conversations.

"Freedom just around the corner for you
But with truth so far off what good will it do?
...Oh, Jokerman."

As Marshal wended his way through the throng of people littering the streets, from boozy nights out or otherwise, he recalled other breakups. Snatches of criticism tumbled out of his memory, like rubbish sacks falling off a dustcart. Tanya said he was too serious. Petra complained he was too glib. They had both been right. "You're dead inside," Rebecca concluded. He was going to counter that it had made him a more efficient killer in Helmand, but he thought it prudent to remain silent. Caroline pointed out that he was the most sarcastic person she had ever met. Marshal took it as a compliment. "You don't care about anyone but yourself," she added, as a parting shot. "That's not fair. I don't particularly care about myself either." He was being sincere rather than sarcastic in his response for once, he thought. "You're forever quoting other people, from all the books you read. Haven't you got anything to say for yourself?" another old flame remarked, wanting to hurt him. Or rather hurt him back. "No, not really."

There's nothing new under the sun.

So many of his girlfriends believed that they could change him – or save him. And then they resented him when he proved them wrong.

Marshal imagined his mother looking down and disapproving of his behaviour. He should be more gentlemanly. But then again, "The Prince of Darkness is a gentleman." Marshal was more of a bastard than a good Catholic, by a comfortable margin. He wondered, however, if he had earned some credit with God through his actions earlier. Even if so, it was unlikely he could have expunged the mountain of venial sin accumulated over the past six months.

Marshal shunted the attractive, wounded image of Alison from his mind's eye by pivoting his thoughts towards the Albanians. He debated whether he had put a fire out, or started one? His mind turned like a rolodex as he mulled over what he knew about Albanian criminal gang culture, from material he had read on the internet and in newspaper articles.

Albanian gangs were rife throughout every major town in Britain (their tentacles also reached into America, Europe,

Asia and the Middle East). They controlled over 50% of the cocaine trade in the country. In London alone, the Albanian mafia was responsible for distributing over half a million kilos of drugs. Their other main focusses of attention were prostitution (they ran the majority of brothels in the capital), people trafficking, money laundering, blackmail and car theft. Their numbers were relatively small, but their impact was significant. The government claimed it was tackling the problem, citing that Albanians formed the third largest group of foreign nationals in its prisons, but they are lies, damn lies and statistics. Each clan was called a *Fis*. The Fis was controlled by an executive committee, a *Barjak* – headed up by a boss, a *Krye*. The krye would pick one or more underbosses, a *Kryetar*, to ensure his orders were carried out. Family ties strengthened the bonds of loyalty in each clan – and made it difficult for the security services to infiltrate the gangs. Members needed to take an oath on joining each gang. A medieval Muslim honour code dictated that blood should be spilled for blood. One gang's motto was, "We are the Gods of the street." Another gang's members were nicknamed "the stabbers". A YouTube video boasted that they were "ready" for war with the police. Marshal read one article which mentioned how Albanian foot-soldiers were heavily into rap culture, which was reason enough to deport or exterminate them. They were also fond of flaunting their wealth and untouchable status on Facebook, posting pictures of rolls of cash or bags of cocaine, carrying guns and knives, wearing designer clothes – the vulgar kind with the names of the brands emblazoned across the garments.

Marshal could research the subject more, but he needed intel outside the public domain, to gain a tactical advantage over his opponents. He needed information specific to the gang he was dealing with, rather than the Albanian mafia in general. He had poked the hornet's nest. Marshal recalled a speech by Churchill, *"This is not the end. It is not even the beginning of the end. But it is, perhaps, the end of the beginning."* He resolved to clean his Glock 21 in the morning.

It was not an unwinnable war, Marshal considered as he returned home and poured himself a large *Talisker*. His shoulder was stiff. Sometimes he thought that a fragment of the bullet was still buried in his flesh. As to sourcing more intelligence, he had a potential solution.

Oliver Porter.

5.

Morning.

Sunlight proliferated through the canopy of birch trees, like water pouring through a colander. Oliver Porter – dressed in a dark blue Barbour jacket, mustard cords, a striped Jermyn Street shirt and chocolate brown fedora from *Locks & Co* – made his way through the wood close to his home, in a village just outside of Windsor. The ex-Guards officer couldn't quite completely shake the military gait out of his stride. It was ingrained, like the catechism. He took in a lungful of the crisp, bracing air. Yellow and green leaves crunched beneath his feet. Porter quoted Keats, *To Autumn*, beneath his breath.

"Season of mists and mellow fruitfulness
Close bosom-friend of the maturing sun
Conspiring with him how to load and bless
With fruit the vines that round the thatch-eves run."

He had more of his life behind him than in front of him, Porter wistfully concluded on his birthday earlier in the year – and decided to re-visit the poets of his youth, including Milton, Chaucer, Tennyson and Virgil. He was particularly fond of Alexander Pope. He grinned, recalling how he had quoted the satirist during an interminable Brexit discussion the other evening, at an equally interminable drinks party. The wine was screw-top, and the host was a human rights lawyer. Unfortunately, the fascists outnumbered the democrats. When someone mentioned that Gina Miller might be attending the party, he physically cringed. Porter was willing to leave the event should she turn-up, even though he was famished, and the canapes were on the way. He could offer his wife their clandestine signal, of him taking off his cufflink and refastening it, and they could be out the house and in the car within three minutes. They were well drilled in the manoeuvre. Porter was asked which side he voted for in the referendum. Surely, he was now wise enough to vote "Remain?" "Have you not seen the light?" the host's wife, an insipid vegan who self-identified with victimised trans people and Polly Toynbee, evangelically exclaimed. He thought he would let Pope answer for him, and quoted his short poem, *The Balance of Europe*.

"Now Europe balanc'd, neither side prevails:
For nothing's left in either of the scales."

Violet, a black and white knee-high mongrel, playfully scampered around him, searching for a suitable stick to gnaw on. Her tail wagged, in a windmill motion, and her ears stood pricked to attention when she occasionally glanced back at him. She was a picture of health and happiness. But it wasn't always so. Every now and then her ears would droop, and Violet would emit a whimper, or pining noise, as she remembered her previous owner. Michael Devlin – a former associate. Devlin had shot himself, with his Sig Sauer P226, shortly after his final hit, around a year ago. Porter had rushed to his apartment that day, suspecting that something was amiss. But it was too late. The ex-soldier was one of the most honourable people Porter had ever known, but the widower was also one of the saddest. At worst he was finally at peace. At best he was with his wife, Holly, in the next life. The two friends had been through a lot together. Devlin had saved Porter's life, after a contract with a couple of London gangsters had gone awry. Before the Parker brothers could get to Porter, Devlin got to them. Yet the officer couldn't save his soldier. Or the soldier had no desire to save himself. Devlin was keen to find a good home for his dog. In some ways, Violet reminded Porter of his burden – and sometimes the mongrel eased it. Perhaps that was his friend's intention. Victoria, Oliver's wife, took the dog in without question or complaint, and she loved Violet upon meeting her for the first time, as if she had loved the creature all her life.

Walking Violet was a staple part of his retirement. The exercise did him good. His face and figure were trim. He still had some of his hair, and not all of it was grey. A recent family holiday in Belize gave his complexion an attractive glow, like a walnut veneer on a piece of antique furniture. He was a picture of health, wealth and happiness. He now just drank two large glasses of wine with dinner, rather than a bottle and a half. His level of smoking – and similarly his blood pressure – had gone down. As well as dog walking, Porter occupied his time with reading, writing (he had just completed a first draft of a novel set in Byzantium at the dawn of the First Crusade) and fishing. He had recently discovered a spot on the Kennett that was a veritable sanctuary, with a nearby pub and no mobile phone reception. Porter also apportioned time to his role as a school governor and serving on the parish council. His fellow council members were slightly suspicious of how the "consultant" had earned his money, but they were all too happy to accept the money when he made significant donations at Christmas and Easter. The gossips and cynics were right to be wary of their convivial, but confounding, neighbour. The consultant worked as a "fixer". Organisations had hired him over the years to make or break political careers. The latter was always easier, given the odious characters who were attracted to the profession, like flies to shit. Porter was adept at finding a person's weak spot, confident as he was that every person had one. Blackmail and bribery were common currency. Sex scandals could be manufactured, but most of the time reality sufficed. If you needed close personal protection, Porter could arrange a professional and discreet bodyguard. If you needed a passport, he would not ask you what it was needed for. Rather he would just ask for which country. If you needed to move your money out of the country, Porter would introduce you to a trusted courier or hawaladar. If you were an unregistered lobbyist, he could arrange a meeting with the appropriate minister, over a cordial lunch for three at the Athenaeum or the Savile Club. If you needed compromising material on an enemy (or friend), then Porter would hire an investigator or hacker on your behalf. He would get his hands dirty, so others wouldn't have to. If you were someone who had capital, but the wrong bloodline, who needed to get a child into the right school, then Porter would just ask the client if they preferred Eton or Harrow.

The respected, respectable Guards officer sat like a spider, at the heart of a web which was connected to the security services, media, the criminal underworld, corrupt corporations and iniquitous individuals. Every problem could be solved, fixed, without fuss or fanfare. For certain distinguished (monied) personages, Porter worked as a broker between clients and associates. Hitmen. Unfortunately, or not, Porter was seldom short of business over the years.

Former satisfied clients would still contact him, but he always courteously said no, when they tried to make him an offer he couldn't refuse. When former associates asked for work, due to burning through money (or divorcing), Porter referred them to private military and security contractors. He was retired – and happier for it.

Porter did have one minor problem he needed to fix today, however. His wife had asked him to arrange a driver and bodyguard for her niece, Grace, who was flying in from New York. Grace was coming back to Britain, having worked as a fashion model in America for a decade. Victoria was fond of her niece. Porter had met Grace a couple of times and he found her charming and intelligent enough. For a model.

The fixer contacted a couple of suitable ex-soldiers he had employed for close protection work before, but they were unavailable. His wife had stressed how the candidate needed to be trustworthy. "I don't want them hitting on Grace. Find someone happily married, if that particular unicorn still exists. Or better still, find someone gay... She's been through a lot this year."

Porter emitted a small sigh, both then and now. He would make some more calls when he got home. The Kennett would have to wait. The fish would have to do without his company this afternoon.

The fixer's attention was temporarily turned away from his task though. One of his neighbours, Henry Troughton, accompanied by his young son, Simon, was approaching from the opposite direction. Porter emitted a slightly wearier sigh, before putting on a smile to greet his fellow school governor. Although they served together on the school board and were neighbours, neither man considered the other a friend.

"I suspect that Henry will never like you, as he cannot forgive you for displacing him as the richest man in the village. Money means the world to him. And you will never like Henry because he is a bore," Victoria had explained to her husband, perceptive as ever.

Troughton, an investment banker and chair of the local Conservative Party Association, was wearing a worsted tweed suit. Apparently, his political hero was Chris Grayling. Much to Porter's displeasure, he noticed that Troughton had on the same *Le Chameau* chasseur style wellington boots. He hoped that was the only thing they had in common. The banker was as jowly and pot-bellied as Porter used to be. He walked with a slight limp, from gout rather than an old war wound. If one was misfortunate enough to get close to his porcine features, one would have noticed broken blood vessels beneath the skin, like tributaries of rivers on a map. The bumptious Tory was self-righteous, without being self-aware. His ambition for the coming year was to install himself on the candidate list to be the next Conservative Party MP for the constituency. He had the time and capital to run a good campaign. Troughton often trumpeted how he was descended from Sir Horace Walpole. Who knew? And who cared? Ironically, the man standing in front of him could have granted the would-be politician his wish, in a previous life. Troughton held more opinions about any and everything than Shami Chakrabarti – and was just as keen as her to get into the House of Lords. Porter felt sorry for his timid, bird-like wife, Margot, who had to suffer the brunt of his overbearing manner. He just hoped that the boy would not be so cowed when he came of age.

"Morning Oliver," Troughton announced, in his bluff, plummy accent.

"Morning Henry."

Violet duly greeted Simon effusively. The boy bent down and stroked the affectionate dog. She rolled over and let him tickle her tummy. Troughton looked down his nose at the mutt and sneered a little. Porter wasn't quite sure if he disliked dogs in general, on just mongrels. Troughton no doubt preferred creatures with a pedigree.

"So, what do you think about the school's latest proposed policy, of offering more bursaries to pupils? It's all trendy, tokenistic codswallop from our new deputy head, no? Don't fix what isn't broke. We should be conscious of retaining our traditions and base," Troughton exclaimed, as if campaigning on the stump. He was keen to secure Porter's support to block the policy.

"A change can be as good as a rest," the influential governor replied, shrugging, knowing that it would vex Troughton to adopt a blasé attitude towards the issue.

"But may I ask how you are intending to vote?"

Porter sighed, internally. He wanted to be on his way back home. Victoria would have a bacon sandwich waiting for him. She would butter him up, as well as the bread, so he would then attend to the onerous task of finding a driver for her niece. He sat on the horns of a dilemma, albeit of the minor kind. Porter didn't want to say he would vote against the policy (God only knew how shallow the gene pool was at the school). But at the same time, if he stated that he was voting for an increase in bursaries, to allow admissions for students with less affluent parents, Troughton would chew his ear off for the next half hour. When, really, Porter just wanted to be chewing on some thick-cut bacon.

The pause grew more pronounced. Even Violet looked his way, waiting for his response.

His phone chimed.

Saved by the bell.

Porter pulled the device out of his pocket and raised an eyebrow at the caller ID displayed on the screen.

James Marshal.

His initial thought was that it was a misdial. He hadn't heard from the ex-Para for several years. Porter pulled out a mental file on his former employee.

James Marshal. From a military family. Served with distinction in Afghanistan with 3 Para. Passed SAS selection, but wounded in Helmand before he could transfer to the Regiment. A cool, or cold, character. A likely depressive, but he hid it well. A misanthrope, but Porter wasn't about to think less of the man for that. A drinker, but a happy one who remained in control of his emotions. Intelligent and sarcastic. Marshal could get himself into trouble and out of it. Unmarried. Womaniser. After leaving the army he had served as a PMC in Afghanistan and Iraq. For the most part, he had been employed as a personal security operative for UK diplomats and government officials. He had also worked a stint for shipping companies, combating Somali pirates. He returned home and was introduced to Porter through a mutual acquaintance. He employed the ex-soldier as a close personal protection officer. He was good at his job. The clients liked him. A couple of female clients liked him a little too much, but at least Marshal was professional enough to screw the women after his contract had ended with them.

After a year of working for him, Porter decided to flirt with the idea of offering Marshal more lucrative work. He could make a killing. Marshal flirted back.

"How much does it pay?"

"You will never have to order the house wine again. I will send some figures over. Each contract is different though... This work is not for everyone. Should you be too overly keen to do it, I will have my doubts about your suitability. But you have killed before in Helmand. You know what it's like to pull the trigger. How did it make you feel?"

"Better I killed them than they killed me or my friends. I didn't lose any sleep over their deaths. Other people got to live, because they died."

"You don't particularly like people, do you James?"

"I can't believe anyone can much like people, after getting to know them. Life is a sexually transmitted disease."

"Life may still be sacred, however. You're a Catholic are you not?"

"I'm lapsed."

Their conversation progressed no further as, shortly after their lunch, Marshal informed his employer that he needed to take an indefinite leave of absence. His grandfather had suffered a stroke and he wanted to take care of him. The last Porter heard was that the grandfather died, and Marshal inherited a chunk of money. Yet perhaps, given his call, Marshal had drunk or gambled away his bequest. Easy come, easy go. Or perhaps the ex-soldier was getting in touch because he had an itch he wanted to scratch. He needed to experience an adrenaline rush again, to help fill the vacuum of civilian life. Lastly, he thought of how James Marshal possessed the same thousand-yard stare as Michael Devlin.

Normally, Porter would have ignored the call. He was retired. If it was important Marshal would call back. But, in order to extricate himself from his exchange with his trying neighbour, he answered the phone.

"I'm terribly sorry Henry, but I have to take this. I am sure I will bump into you again soon," he said warmly, hoping to God that he wouldn't. "If not, I will see you at the next board meeting... Porter speaking."

"Morning Oliver. I hope I'm not disturbing you."

"No. It's fine to talk," he replied, after sighing with relief on seeing Troughton walk away. He wasn't the worst Tory he knew, but that wasn't saying much.

"I need to ask a favour," Marshal posited, straightforward yet polite.

"As long as you will be okay if I say no, ask away."

Marshal proceeded to describe, without fanfare or fuss, his altercation with the Albanians the day before. Porter listened. Whether it was with sympathy or disinterest, Marshal couldn't rightly tell. Occasionally he would interject and ask a point of enquiry.

"Do they know where you live, or were they able to take your picture?"

"No."

After hearing Marshal's succinct report, Porter thought him either brave or stupid for challenging the Albanians. Or brave *and* stupid. He could well have dug a hole for himself. Yet he was prepared to keep on digging, given the favour he was asking. Marshal wanted information on the gang who were looking to move into the neighbourhood. Did Porter's associates still have access to the NCA and other relevant databases? Marshal had a name to put into the system. He would happily pay the required rate for any services rendered.

"I will not charge you a fee for any information James, but I would ask a favour from you in return."

Not only did Porter not want to receive any money for his labour (as he was retired, and a fee would turn him into a professional "fixer" again), but he would no longer have to suffer the onerous duty of searching for a driver for his wife's niece.

Problem solved.

6.

God had his hand on the dimmer switch, and he was turning it. Cars began to turn on their bulbous headlights. Pedestrians began to regret wearing their summer wardrobes. The sickly green Thames undulated, its eddies causing the surface to seemingly resemble reptilian scales. Tufts of foam spotted the river, like the white spittle or scum which can accrue in the corner of a mouth.

Marshal walked over Westminster Bridge, on his way to meet Oliver Porter at the National Liberal Club, just off Whitehall. He had received a text a couple of hours after their phone call. Porter would be able to obtain the information he asked for. He would come into London and give it to him personally, as well as discuss the favour Marshal would grant him in return.

Buses juddered, as if shivering from the cold. Taxi drivers moaned about Uber. Horns blared, rippling the air. The bridge was thick with Yahoos and Morlocks – and, worse, cyclists, Marshal mused. There were too many wrap-around sunglasses on display. Too many Birkenstocks. Not enough paperback books were poking out of handbags or jacket pockets. Marshal lit another cigarette and worked his way through the forest of selfie-sticks and inane, giggling tourists. Negotiating the obstacle course on SAS selection was easier – and less irritating – he fancied.

Marshal decided to walk from his home in order to smoke more and collect his thoughts. Perhaps Porter was right. He advised taking a holiday. Disappear. Allow things to blow over. But, be it through pride or not, the soldier had no intention of retreating. He couldn't let the Albanians win, like the Taliban. It would stick in his craw too much. He hoped that the intelligence Porter was gathering could give him a tactical advantage. He didn't just want to evade the enemy, like a fox staying ahead of the hounds. He wanted to take the fight to them.

After finishing his conversation with Marshal earlier in the day, Porter contacted one of his old associates, Mariner. A hacker. There were few systems he couldn't access, foreign or domestic. MI6 sometimes employed him, as it was better the hacker worked for them rather than their rivals. Mariner was still an enigma to Porter. He suspected he had mild Asperger's. He still lived with his mother in the basement of her house. All he knew for sure, which was the only thing worth knowing, was that Mariner always delivered. There would be an additional charge for prioritising the job, but the hacker could complete the task by the end of the afternoon. Mariner made good on his word. Porter checked the draft folder on old email account they shared – so there was no actual emailing of material – to find a wealth of intelligence on Vasil Bisha and the organisation he was affiliated with. Porter then sent Marshal a text to confirm their meeting.

"Would you like the good news or the bad news?" he said to his wife.

"The bad news."

"I've got to head into London, for a meeting."

"And the good news?"

"It looks like I may have found a driver for Grace."

"That's great news. Thank you, darling. Occasionally you still remind me of why I stay married to you," she jested, flashing a smile that still made Porter's day, even after decades of being wed. "The children are staying with friends for a few days. Will you be coming back home for dinner later, or staying the night in town?"

"What's on the menu? Salad or something else?"

"Roast pork, with chestnut stuffing and goose fat potatoes."

"I'll be home for dinner. Sometimes you remind me why I remain married to you too."

"Flattery will get you everywhere. You may even get lucky tonight."

"In that case, I'll try to get the earlier train," Porter replied, smiling – feeling lucky already.

"I've said to Grace that she can stay with us for a few days. I did not want her staying in some hotel, alone."

"That's fine. I may be able to arrange for her prospective driver to stay in the guesthouse, so he will be on hand for her."

Porter, having glanced over the material from Mariner, considered that Marshal could now have a target on his back, whether the weapon of choice would be a blade or bullet. If they chose to, the Albanians had the manpower to reconnoitre the neighbour. Once they found out his name or address, Porter would suffer a severe beating, at best. The Albanians believed in blood for blood. An honour code amongst thieves.

He further studied the intelligence on the train to London and was further convinced that it was best Marshal vacate his home for a week or so. He also called the National Liberal Club to reserve a table, enjoying having a first class carriage to himself.

He hailed a cab when he got to Paddington station and reached the club in good time. The journey had taken less than two hours, door to door. But still, London felt distant, like it was another world. Sparkling. Unpleasant. Righteous. Irreligious. Ignoble. Yes, more than anything else, ignoble. He could feel the selfishness and ignorance clogging up the air, choking him like the diesel fumes from the traffic.

Porter walked up the curving, marble staircase and through the opulent clubrooms, full of burnished mahogany furniture and deep-pile carpets. He told himself that the portraits of Rosebery and Churchill no longer gazed at him with such disapproval, now he was retired.

The National Liberal Club was established by William Gladstone in 1882. The neo-Gothic building sat close to the river, between Embankment tube and Whitehall. The club was meant to furnish members with "a home for democracy, devoid of class." Marshal would have been sceptical whether it had done so in the nineteenth century. He was even more doubtful it met the criteria in the twenty-first. Winston

Churchill and G. K. Chesterton had been members, but so had, unfortunately, Nick Clegg and George Bernard Shaw. Shockingly, the club did not admit women members until the 1970s. Depressingly, it was the first of the major London clubs to do so.

Marshal entered the dining room and surveyed the scene. He had been a member of similar gentleman's clubs over the years – and felt half at home. Although he felt more at home now in a local pub. The white linen table cloths gleamed, matching the mainly white faces occupying the chamber. Some of the tables were empty, and some full. Glasses were chinked together in various toasts. Cutlery clinked against plates. A burst of laughter exploded from a party of half a dozen fifty-somethings in the corner, who were rounding off their lunch with some ruby port. The smell of wine and roasted meat livened up his nostrils. Marshal recalled a dinner his father had arranged at the club, many years ago. The room had been a fug of tobacco smoke back then (from cigarettes, cigars and even one pipe), before people became miserable and a new puritanism set in. Ostensibly the evening was just a friendly, informal get together. But shortly before the young officer took his seat around the long table his father mentioned how he had organised the meal in order for his son to network and further his career. "Make it a successful night." It was, in so far as a lissom Polish waitress, with a love of Chopin and halter tops, gave him her number by the close of the dinner. Marshal was unsure as to whether his career had progressed or not.

As he was shown to Porter's table, Marshal noticed a rare sight – a Liberal Democrat MP. They were a veritable endangered species. But ultimately, they were cockroaches. They could survive a nuclear holocaust, a fate second only to Brexit, the member for Eastbourne might argue. He overheard a few words of conversation as he passed by the MP and his guests: "Plebs... arbitrage... pension... House of Lords."

Porter rose to his feet on seeing his guest. At first, Marshal did not quite recognise him, given the weight he had lost. The ex-Guards officer was wearing a creaseless tan coloured suit, from *Brooke's Brothers*. His shoes, from *Foster & Son*, were polished to parade ground standard, as was his silver tie pin. Marshal had never seen his former employer dressed anything but immaculately. Porter once admitted to owning a pair of jeans, but he may have said so for effect. Marshal couldn't say he was ever particularly close to the fixer – or could wholly trust him. If Porter was a book then he was one with some of the pages deliberately torn out or redacted, to obscure the story. His family life was private, in relation to his business contacts. Doubtless, his wife was ignorant, as to how he earned his living. He had ruined the lives of innocent and guilty people alike, arranging honeytraps, financial scandals and contract killings. Yet he was the soul of civility, whilst committing all manner of ignominious acts. Porter paid his employees on time, always picked up the tab, gave generously to charity (autonomous of tax breaks), quoted Trollope, hummed Elgar and, to Marshal's knowledge, he had never been unfaithful to his wife. Porter was always entertaining company, but Marshal judged that his life had not suffered for being out of contact with the fixer. But he needed his help now, even at the expense of owing the man, who he had once nicknamed "Talleyrand", a favour.

Needs must.

"James, it's good to see you again. I wish it could be under more felicitous circumstances," Porter remarked, shaking Marshal's hand, offering him a smile which was as attractive as his suit.

"We are where we are," the ex-Para replied, quoting a familiar phrase from his time in the army.

Porter took in his dinner companion, his eyes briefly narrowing in scrutiny, like two pill-box slits. Marshal was wearing a charcoal grey suit and black tie. He could have been on his way to a funeral. His own, if the Albanians had anything to do with things, Porter half-joked. He was cleanshaven and still in good shape. A couple of the waitresses – and one of the waiters – had already gazed at him with more than a modicum of interest and appreciation. Porter noted a lack of a wedding ring and slightly bloodshot eyes. He could smell smoke on his breath, but his fingers were free from nicotine stains.

"Mr Porter, it's good to see you again," Alessio, one of the long-serving waiters at the club, remarked, as he approached the table. The grey-haired, amiable Florentine seemed genuinely pleased to see the member – and not just because, whether he ordered a coffee or three-course meal, Porter always left a £50 tip for the staff. "We haven't seen you for some time, I believe."

"I no longer venture to town so regularly. I'm retired. As much as I might miss your cutlets and selection of whiskies, I don't miss the commute."

Alessio's camp, cherubic face broke into an obliging smile and he raised his pen and notepad.

"Can I interest you in a glass of wine?"

"No, but you can interest us in a bottle," Porter replied.

7.

Porter handed over the flash drive containing the intelligence Mariner had mined from an array of sources. He spoke calmly, discreetly, with an amenable expression – as if he were discussing his plans for Christmas, or a recent trip to Lord's cricket ground.

"The information is comprehensive, but that may be part of the problem. The organisation is formidable and vicious. I am not usually given to quoting Donald Trump, but you have got yourself mixed up with some "bad hombres" James. The gang, which took over the drug and prostitution trades of over half of Glasgow, are now intent on establishing themselves in South London. Their krye is one Luka Rugova. He is not known for his clemency. He may view that you attacked a member of his family, and therefore committed an act of war. You may need to worry about his lieutenant, Viktor Baruti, even more, however. He's as intelligent as he is ruthless. Read the files. Baruti seems to be an adherent of Stalin's philosophy, given the number of murders his name has been attributed to. "Death is the solution to all problems. No man. No problem." If it seems like I'm trying to scare you, it's because I am. I would not think less of you – and nor should you think less of yourself – if you chose to disappear, before Baruti causes you to disappear."

Marshal's half-smile didn't falter. His shrug seemed genuinely insouciant, rather than for show. Marshal was also a Para, as well as philosophical. Resilient. Paras, officers and squaddies, were used to enduring, being outnumbered and fighting against the odds. Churchill had founded the regiment in 1942. They were "men apart". The first to fight and the last to leave the battlefield.

"I am grateful for the intelligence Oliver. I'll judge the lay of the land this evening and tomorrow," he replied, clutching the flash drive as if it were a gem. Or key. He didn't want to commit to either evading or engaging the enemy at present. With a subtle flick of his eyes, he conveyed to Porter that Alessio was approaching, to refill their glasses.

"Can I ask, what made you want to confront the Albanians in the first place?" Porter asked, after the waiter was safely out of earshot.

"I'm not sure. Like most things in life, there are more questions than answers. Maybe it was due to the fact that they were dealing with impunity, just a stone's throw away from a school. Perhaps I've read too much William Blake. Against my better judgement, I still believe in innocence – however fleeting it may be. Or I believe in justice, and they deserved to be punished. Somebody had to do something. I was either in the right or wrong place. Time will tell. The police seem to have better things to do, like tweet, than clean-up the crime on our streets. I am willing to go places the police can't. I'll soon be familiar with their personnel and operation. But they still don't know who I am, or what I am capable of," Marshal argued, his features tightening in determination. Yet his half-smile seemed to widen rather than diminish.

"Well, I hope you're still capable of doing me a favour, as per our agreement."

"Go on," Marshal replied, partly concentrating on the people he saw on the terrace outside, smoking. Desiring to join them. He was also briefly distracted by a querulous fifty-something old woman, who was complaining that her steak had been overcooked. She seemed to be enjoying the attention she was attracting – and spoke to the staff as if they were Untermensch.

"I told you I wanted my steak blue. Blue! Do you not know what that means? Did you not write it down? You silly girl! I have been coming to this club for years, since before you were born. I know people at the BBC."

Her intention was to intimidate but, more so, she proved to be a source of amusement for staff and diners alike. She smelled of lavender and mouldy old newspaper. *The Guardian*, no doubt. She looked like a grey-haired Cherie Blair, although Marshal fancied that her husband was more scrupulous and faithful. The shrill harridan, who had spent the morning shopping at Debenham's and then popped into a refugee charity she was a patron of, also distracted Porter, but he nevertheless ploughed on with things.

"I just need you to drive my niece around for a few days. According to my wife her schedule involves a few meetings in West London. A friend of hers is also hosting a party in some country pile, near Oxford. I need someone I can trust, and therefore put my wife's mind at ease. Her name is Grace. She is a former fashion model, back from living in New York. Apparently, she has had some bad boyfriends in the past couple of years, although that may be a tautology. All boyfriends are bad, if you're a father. I will need you to keep any dealings with Grace on a strictly professional level. I do not want you trying to make a play for her. I'm ambivalent, but my wife is adamant about that – and one should always do what one's wife says. The only codicil to the job is that you will need to be at her beckoned call, so to speak. I'm happy to put you up in our guesthouse. The job should last more than a couple of days, but no longer than a week."

Marshal remained impassive, as if he were sitting for his passport photo. But he knew he had to assent to Porter's request. He had no other way of obtaining the intelligence he needed. It was a price worth paying. He had played the role of a driver before. There was nothing new under the sun. He would tug his forelock and say, "Yes Mam" and "No Mam" to the would-be princess. She would be far too self-obsessed to grant him a second-look. If he could be indifferent to God, Marshal was sure he could be capable of indifference towards a retired fashion model.

"When do I start?"

The office of the nightclub, *The High Life*, had blacked out windows, which looked down onto the dancefloor and main bar. The club was situated between Camberwell and Kennington. Luka Rugova refurbished the venue shortly after making it his base of London operations. He installed plenty of intimate booths, chrome fittings and new toilets, decked out in black marble, so the clientele could easily see any remnants of their coke. There wasn't a single square foot of carpet in the establishment, given how difficult it was to remove blood and wine stains from it. The club served food, Balkan and Western cuisine, and stayed open till three in the morning (although, for employees and business associates, it was open twenty-four hours). The club was a success, even if you discounted the product which was moved through it and its value as a money laundering operation.

Luka Rugova sat behind his desk in the office. Viktor Baruti sat on a nearby armchair, answering messages on his phone. Vasil Bisha and Tarin Bashkim stood in the middle of the room, looking more than a little nervous and cowed. Across the other side of the room, curled up on a large leather sofa, were two prostitutes, half sleeping and half high. They hadn't slept the night before – and had still provided hospitality for a couple of business associates of Rugova's during the morning and afternoon. Ferid, the krye's driver and bodyguard, sat Buddha-like on another sofa in the corner. A serene, or sated, expression, softened his features. His double chin was buried in his chest, as if he were on the cusp of falling asleep. Dandruff covered the square shoulders of his suit, like a dusting of snow on tarmac. Gold rings hung off his sausage fingers. His lips were pink, rubbery. His flat nose, which given his bull-like appearance and build, wouldn't have looked out of place with a ring through it. Ferid was fiercely loyal, as well as just being fierce, when called upon. He had known his employer since childhood and had beaten more men to a pulp than he cared to remember. The office was also home to a pool table, safe, metal cabinet and mini-bar, which ran along half the side of the back wall. A large, heavily tinted window overlooked the carpark, which housed Rugova's crimson Bentley, Baruti's black Lexus and Bisha's silver Subaru XV.

A view voices could be heard downstairs as the bar staff began to arrive, their heels clicking against the polished wooden floor. The kitchen was already in gear and the smell of *qebapa* wafted through the building.

A computer, printer and bust of Napoleon sat on Rugova's large, teak desk – along with a full ashtray, next to flecks of cocaine. A catalogue, containing small yachts for sale, was open in front of him. The krye was flirting with the idea of buying a boat, to moor outside his villa in Vlora. The boat could be used for smuggling, and family holidays. The attractive, impressive antique desk had once belonged to Bajram Curri, a hero of Albania who had fought for the country's independence at the beginning of the twentieth century. He had died, committing suicide, rather than be captured by enemy forces. A couple of empty bottles of Cristal champagne and a half-eaten plate of *tave kosi* could also be found on the desk. On the wall, next to the krye, hung a huge painting of Skanderbeg, Lord of Albania – a fifteenth-century prince and military commander who helped unite the Albanians and successfully fought against the Ottoman Empire. He was famed for having personally killed thousands of men on the battlefield. His coat of arms, featuring the double-headed eagle, formed the basis of the Albanian flag. The portrait, specially commissioned by the krye, depicted the bearded nobleman brandishing a bloodied sword, slaying his enemies. A landscape of Rugova's coastal hometown also hung on the wall. As much as the Albanian was forging a life – and empire – for himself in the new world, he often spared a thought for his home and its traditions too.

He finished reading an email and focused his attention on his two errant employees, pursing his lips in disappointment. Grey hairs marked his temples, increasing his lupine appearance. His skin was stretched across his face, giving rise to the rumour that the forty-year-old regularly received Botox injections. Yet no one understandably owned the audacity to broach the issue with him. An inch-long tattoo of a knife could be seen on his neck. His otherwise black hair was slicked back, with grease or hair gel. His build was lithe, athletic, as opposed to bulky. He didn't want to give off the impression of being a thug. He was a businessman. Rugova wore an Armani suit, Boss silk shirt (with the top two buttons undone) and Gucci loafers. A gold chain and pendant, of a scimitar, hung around his neck – a gift from his mother. A triangular-shaped scar, over his left eyebrow, had been a gift from his father – a month before the abused fourteen-year-old boy had murdered him, with a scimitar.

As much as the issue in front of him was an unwelcome irritation, the Albanian's hostile takeover was proceeding as planned. He had not trespassed on Russian or Chinese territory, but the West Indian and independents were fair game in South London. He had flooded the area with cheap product, using new and old gang members to establish and enforce his franchise. The West Indians were in retreat, although far from defeated. Once his product dominated the market, he would raise prices accordingly. The pink pound and city boys in the area were a particularly lucrative revenue stream. It amused him how half his crew were scornful of the gays, but the other half were keen to sell to them. Rugova was happy for his men to fraternise with the kafirs. To get high with them, to get into bed with them. Their money was good, that was the main thing. He was a businessman first, a Muslim second. The grey pound was on the rise too. Old men were the principal clients in their brothels, spread across Soho, Lambeth and Southwark. Most preferred the older whores, even if they were dried-up and had missing teeth. It was just a matter of lowering the prices, depending on the quality, or lack of quality, of the merchandise. The hags were still assets.

Business was good. The club, and other small enterprises he owned, washed the money. His alliance with the local Turks was strong. Once he was strong enough, he would turn them into the junior partners in the relationship. Hiring personnel from other Balkan states, as opposed to just Albanians, had proved an astute move and plugged a hole in their labour shortage (he still needed to keep his foot on the throat of things up in Scotland too). Rugova was due to receive another shipment of girls next week, which he would farm out to the Hellbanianz in East London and their brothels in Southend.

The move from Glasgow had not all been plain sailing though. The krye had to put down a few markers, make an example of rivals. But the deaths, amputations and castrations had served their purpose. For some reason, he had been rumoured to give a couple of his competitors a Columbian necktie. Notwithstanding that it was a physical impossibility to cut someone's throat and pull their tongue through the gash, he let the rumour spread.

The police had also tried – and failed – to check his success. Their second, fruitless raid would probably be their last though. The kyre was conscious of only keeping a minimal amount of product on the premises, so the most they could prosecute someone for was for possession, rather than intent to supply. They thought they scored when they discovered several shotguns and knives in the metal cabinet in his office. But the shotguns were licenced, for hunting, and his lawyer argued that the knives were for use in the club's kitchen. Baruti had arranged for a couple of police to be on the payroll, who would provide him with valuable intelligence. Rugova had also put a warning shot across the detective's bow, who had dared to go after him. The DI's name was Martin Elmwood. He thought he was a bulldog, but he was a mewling pup. The krye had set him straight, defiantly looking him in the eye as the policeman stood in his office. Smirking as he taunted/threatened him.

"I am just a businessman. I would advise you to treat me as a businessman, rather than a criminal. I am not your enemy, but a potential ally. The West Indians are your enemies. Pimps exploiting diseased whores and dealers cutting their coke with laundry detergent are your enemies… If you do not come knocking on my door, I will have no need to come knocking on yours. And, trust me Detective Inspector, you do not want me knocking on your door in the middle of the night and disturbing you and your family. Your wife, Karen, and your two young children, Peter and Kelly."

But Rugova knew he had to be careful, vigilant. London wasn't Glasgow. Special Branch were not the Scottish police. If he put his head above the parapet too much, he would become more of a target. The underworld should remain underground.

Rugova took another drag on his cigarette and placed it back in the ashtray.

"Perhaps I should hire the man who did this to you. You say the stranger was an Englishman," the krye remarked. Despite the prospective Botox injections, his forehead was wrinkled in dismay or denigration.

Bisha and Bashkim stood to attention, as if they were back in the army, despite their weary frames. The two men had taken themselves off to King's College Hospital, after the attack. They headed back to Bisha's flat after being patched-up, dulling the pain with the painkillers the doctor prescribed – and other drugs he didn't. They woke up late the following day and arranged to report to their superiors later in the afternoon. They had explained over the phone how the stranger had caught them unawares. Bisha replayed the scene in his mind, envisioning other outcomes. Bashkim, his crooked face contorted in malice, imagined torturing their assailant. The Englishman had been lucky before. He wouldn't get the chance to be lucky again, he promised – grunting to himself. Bashkim had a cast on his leg, from a broken ankle. His chin was marked with stitches and a hefty bruise. He leaned on his crutches, his palms slick with sweat, feeling both ridiculous and scared. He had never let his krye down before. His pride seemed shredded. A graze, covering half his face like the mask of the Phantom of the Opera, testified that Bisha had been in the wars too. He waited for his krye's judgement. At least the attack had not turned into a robbery. Loss of income was worse than loss of life. His eyes flitted towards Baruti, who he was equally keen not to upset. Unfortunately, Bisha couldn't help but stare at the two whores on the sofa – and lick his lips. One, the bottle blonde, was wearing a mauve sequined dress. A rock of cocaine hung from her left nostril. Her scrawny legs were open, and he noticed how she wasn't wearing any underwear. The brunette next to her was wearing black, wet-look leather trousers that seemed so tight, he fancied that she would have to be cut out of them. Her cherry lipstick was smudged, as if it had been applied by a monkey or drunk. As hypnotised as Bisha was by the sight of the two vulnerable girls on the sofa, his head snapped back to attention to answer his krye. It was unspoken that he, as opposed to his guileless companion, would do the talking.

"Yes, I think so," Bisha replied, whilst scratching his crotch.

"You think so, or you know so?"

The voice was as hard and sharp as flint. The kryetar had barely glanced at the two men since they entered, as he concentrated more on replying to emails on his phone. Bisha and Bashkim. Little and large. They were a double act. An unsuccessful one. Baruti's eyes narrowed. A chill ran down Bisha's spine. He had witnessed a similar expression on the kryetar's face previously, just before he shot someone. Or hammered a chisel into a man's hand, after strapping him to a chair. Or when he stuffed a pool ball down someone's throat. Or used a penknife to repeatedly stab the throat of a gang member who had been embezzling. Accusation and thinly veiled contempt lined the enforcer's features, as if carved in stone.

"I know so. Sorry. Yes. He was English," he answered, stammering. His throat became dry and forehead perspired, as Baruti's dark eyes seem to bore into his soul.

If Vasil Bisha had been familiar with the painting, he might have noticed that his kryetar looked like Thomas Phillips' portrait of Byron. The curly black hair was the same, as was the determined, cleft chin. Attractiveness allied to intelligence. Defiance and desire infused his haunted – and haunting – aspect. But not sexual desire. Rather a brooding, sadistic desire. Bisha gulped slightly as his attention was drawn to the gun in the shoulder holster Baruti wore, beneath his jacket. A bribe to an Albanian diplomat meant that the assassin had been granted a licence to carry a firearm.

Before his national service, Baruti had been a student of advanced mathematics. There was something the youth appreciated about the certainty and preciseness of mathematics. Mathematics never lied. As a student, he also read philosophy – and had a few articles on Nietzsche and Schopenhauer published in respected journals. The army changed him, however. Viktor Baruti grew to despise humanity – and considered himself a superior being. Remorse was a disease, which he had somehow been inoculated against at birth. The intellectual wanted to become a man of action. He read Dostoyevsky's *Crime and Punishment* with fervent enthusiasm. Raskolnikov was superior too. The laws – of the state and human nature – shouldn't apply to him. The young Baruti was suitably disappointed when the Russian student experienced guilt for his crimes. Dostoyevsky had only got things half right. Baruti, who had trained as a sniper, would feel no such guilt, he vowed. After leaving the army he played a part and ingratiated himself into a criminal gang. When the opportunity arose, he grasped his chance, and carried out his first murder. His victim was an old sot, who refused to pay his debts. A message needed to be sent out, for others who might be tempted not to pay. Baruti crept-up behind the drunk, used a cut-throat razor and slit his throat from ear to ear. The curve in the wound mirrored the killer's grin. He felt like a vet, putting a mangy animal out of its misery. When he returned home, after completing the hit, the young man sat down to supper with his mother as if it were any other day. He even elected to cook pancakes and washed-up the dishes. He felt like singing, but he didn't. That evening Baruti stayed up late, not wracked with guilt, or reliving the event. Instead, he planned his next hit. His only regret was that he didn't get to look his victim in the eye, as his life was extinguished. He was intrigued as to what fresh death would look like. The killer seldom repeated the error. Over the years Baruti observed shock, resignation, terror, tranquillity and defiance in the aspects of those he executed. But it all added up to the same thing. Death was the ultimate absolute, the only necessary and sufficient property germane to life. Baruti realised he had a talent, as did others. Violence was a commodity, to buy or sell like anything else. Contract after contract was fulfilled, until he found permanent employment as Rugova's kryetar. It was a fine thing to get paid for what you were good at – and loved. The two men, who trusted each other like brothers, worked together in Albania and Glasgow. And now a patch of London was ripe for the taking.

Baruti lived alone, in an apartment at Canada Water, close to the river. The flat was always immaculate, as if the owner had moved in a week ago. He seldom spent any time there though. Life was work. Work was life. Even if it was the dead of night, Baruti would respond to a phone call or text message. The lieutenant oversaw all aspects of the business. The devil is in the detail. A near eidetic memory meant he didn't have to write much down. Rugova gave his loyal lieutenant free rein, in relation to matters of personnel, strategy and accounting. Together they were greater than the sum of their parts.

Baruti woke at 7.00. He would run for an hour each morning and then perform fifty sit-ups and fifty press-ups, before taking an ice-cold shower. He didn't smoke, drink or sample any product. His one indulgence was coffee. He had bought two *La Marzocco* coffee machines. One for his apartment and one for the club. His wardrobe consisted of ten black suits, ten white shirts, ten white polo shirts and ten black tracksuit bottoms. Baruti suffered from OCD. He would be forever straightening his cutlery at the dinner table and, no matter how late it was, would clean and maintain his coffee machine (and gun) before he went to bed.

The kryetar was asexual. He would allow women to give him a massage or manicure, but he considered them to be unhygienic – and duplicitous. He recoiled when he thought of being intimate with a woman. Sex was an animalistic act. Debasing. He had no desire to contract another man's diseases through a woman. Women bred weakness. The whores in the corner held no temptation for him. Even virgins weren't virginal. Desire and abstinence were both a matter of will – and Baruti considered himself master of his own will.

He had once been in a relationship with a fellow mathematician in his youth. Sophia appreciated the elegance of numbers, and never asked anything of him – materially or emotionally. She could be as cold as him, which somehow fomented a mutual warmth. Their relationship was based on a passion for intellectualism, rather than carnality. But Sophia moved away.

The killer's disciplined, yet eccentric, lifestyle gave cause to him earning the nickname "the Mad Monk." Although an atheist, the teachings of the Koran left their mark on the Muslim.

"Be not weak hearted in pursuit of the enemy... Slay them wherever you find them, and drive them out of the places whence they drove you out... If thou comest on them in war, deal with them so as to strike fear in those who are behind them, that they may remember."

As per his ritual, Viktor Baruti stirred his coffee four times and then tapped the spoon against the side of the cup twice.

"I want to clarify events. Be clear in your answers. The Englishman approached and asked you to drive off, because you were dealing?"

"Yes," Bishka asserted, nodding his scabby head, to further emphasise his certainty.

"What did this man look like?"

"He was about six foot. Short, brown hair. Well dressed, in a blue suit."

"Any facial hair, glasses or distinguishing features?"

"No."

"Did he have an accent?"

"He was well spoken. But he had a slight London accent. Yes."

Bishka felt like he was standing under a hot lamp, as Baruti fixed his unforgiving gaze upon him. He would have preferred it if a gypsy gave him the evil eye. He was still scared, lest the kryetar suddenly pulled his gun from his holster. As when he pulled his gun, he usually used it. It wouldn't matter if he was undeserving of any punishment. Bishka recalled a scene when, accompanying Baruti, he had drawn his pistol and pointed it at the head of a dealer who was suspected of skimming from the weekly take. "I am innocent, I swear," the dealer protested, his voice and body trembling, as he kneeled in a pool of his own urine. "I don't believe in innocence," Baruti had casually replied, pulling the trigger. The man's head exploded like a watermelon.

"Whoever he is, he's now a marked man. If somebody attacks you, they attack me. Blood must be paid in blood. It's the code," Rugova flatly argued. He had a duty to his men and liked to promote a culture of fraternity. Family. "Can you look into this? I've got to be off shortly."

The krye wanted to leave. He had arranged to visit his girlfriend, Mona, a mixed-raced model and aspiring actress. He had just installed her in a new apartment, in Greenwich. He wanted to see what he was paying for. He had told her to buy a large HD TV, for when he wanted to watch the football. He would fuck her and then leave. His wife was cooking his favourite, *comlek*, this evening – and he promised his children he would be home early, to take them to the cinema. The krye prided himself on being a man of his word. It was good for business.

"I'll fix it," Baruti stated. Each word punctured the air, like a nail being hammered into the wall. The Englishman, at present, was an anomaly. If he had been contracted by one of their competitors to send a message, then why not mention who the message was from? Or was he just a would-be local hero? Was he ex-police or ex-military? It took someone trained, or deranged, to take on someone of Bashkim's size and best him in such a way. Things didn't quite add up at the moment, but he vowed to solve the equation. If he willed it, the Englishman was as good as dead already.

8.

Marshal woke-up early, restless and dehydrated. After the wine, he had hit the cognac at the club. He had decided not to go through Porter's files the night before, as he wanted to do so with a clear head. In order to sweat the toxins out of his system, he went for an hour's run around Kennington Park.

Dawn stirred and glowed. Or blushed. The colour reminded Marshal of the maroon beret of the Parachute Regiment. A wave of nostalgia, or something more stoical or uplifting, came over him as his feet pounded asphalt and grass. Porter had asked him at dinner if he missed being in the military. During WWII, Montgomery had called the Paras, "men apart." Porter was also aware of the quote, that the Paras were "uniformed psychopaths" too. Marshal replied that he didn't miss the drilling, food or being told what to do. But he did miss something about soldiering. "I'm just not quite sure what."

Marshal let himself recover in the park and returned to his flat. His senses were alert, as if he were entering a hostile environment, with possible snipers or IEDs. Marshal was conscious of surveying the street for any watchers before entering his building. He couldn't let the enemy know where he was based. He showered and fired-up his laptop, inserting the flash drive.

The files were numerous and varied, drawn from the NCA, the Met and agencies north of the border. Marshal was used to gathering and evaluating intelligence, whether it be in relation to Somali pirates, poppy growers in Helmand or kidnap gangs in Baghdad. Marshal first opened the files pertinent to the gang's krye, Luka Rugova, and his activities in Scotland.

Rugova had been a rising star in the Albanian mafia in Tirana. He was granted the go-ahead to commence operations in Glasgow. He was given scope to recruit his own personnel and grow his franchise as he saw fit. He flooded the market with cheap product, which was also superior, purer. He forged alliances with rivals but proved aggressive in dealing with any competitors who defied or attacked him. When Rugova retaliated, he did so with disproportionate force. He would torch his enemies' base of operations and murder key operatives in their homes. Rival gang members were snatched and tortured. Executed. *Shock and awe.* The underworld was a vicious place, but Rugova made it his home. The crime boss naturally came to the attention of the authorities, as well as other gangs. The police perennially lacked hard evidence and witnesses who would testify. Drug-related deaths increased by over 50% in his area of operations, during the course of one year. By the time the police and competitors knew they were in a war with Rugova, he had already won it.

As well as controlling over half the drugs and human trafficking trades in Glasgow the Albanian built-up a significant network of "legitimate" business interests, to launder his money and generate alternative revenue streams. Marshal glanced over the list of businesses he owned (or was purported to own). Although *The High Life* was registered in his own name, Rugova arranged proxy owners for other outlets. Between London and Glasgow, he owned bakeries, restaurants, bars, dry cleaners and a scrap metal yard. He had also ploughed his money into property. It was estimated that the Albanian owned over fifty flats in and around both cities. Some were rented out to legitimate tenants, some housed employees.

An addendum file to one report ran through Rugova's modus operandum for acquiring assets. He would target a business (usually one which he could distribute product through and launder cash) and buy a share in it. Eventually, he would force the original owner out, through intimidation or a buy-out clause, and set-up a proxy with a small offshore holding company to take control of things. Rugova was ruthless – and tax efficient.

An NCA profile stated that the Albanian was charming, when the occasion called for it, and intelligent. His English was excellent and, unlike other Albanian crime bosses,

Rugova mixed outside of his immediate criminal circle. He gave to charity and even did a stint coaching his son's football team. Both Rugova and his wife were neighbourly. They regularly hosted dinner parties in their townhouse in Blackheath (although the krye also hosted slightly less civilised gatherings at his nightclub, with cocaine and escorts in tow, for his gang members and business partners). Rugova had a string of mistresses, but he always kept business and pleasure separate in that regard. He was too smart, cautious, to fall for any honeytrap, one report concluded. He engendered loyalty (each gang member swore an oath of loyalty to the krye) and remunerated his associates well. Undercover operatives, in Glasgow and London, had failed to infiltrate the gang in any meaningful way. Low-level associates had been arrested and successfully prosecuted, but the police had been unable to turn the foot-soldiers against their general. For those gang members who were serving a jail sentence, a report stated that Rugova still looked after them. Drugs, mobile phones and even McDonald's had been smuggled into prisons.

The bulk of the Albanian's business – and revenue – was still centred around cocaine, despite recent diversification. It was a multi-million-pound operation. Their distribution and sales had shifted in the past couple of years. Instead of targeting working-class areas, they focussed on selling to the middle-classes. Young professionals paid more for their product. Rugova's gang had contacts which pushed drugs within the City, Millwall FC, the London Assembly and Channel Four. Technology and diverse supply chains were utilised. Customers could order product, and have it delivered to them as easily as they could order a pizza. Distribution had been expanded and outsourced. Teen gangs were employed to deliver to the door. Rugova had been one of the pioneers of the County Lines system. It didn't seem to matter to the middle-classes that, while they were getting high, youths (usually non-whites) were being stabbed and shot in ongoing turf wars. London was bleeding. And who knew or who cared about the people suffering and dying in their droves in the likes of

Mexico and Columbia? Ignorance – and getting high off cocaine – seemed to be bliss, Marshal mused.

He lit another cigarette and clicked on a file devoted to surveillance photos of their – his – target. Marshal wanted to know what his enemy looked like, as a boxer might pin a picture of his next opponent onto his mirror, to focus and inspire him. With his black hair, tanned skin and designer clothes Rugova resembled a George Michael tribute act. A bad one. A few photos, taken whilst the subject was sunbathing next to his swimming pool, revealed his heavily tattooed body. His torso was swathed in ink. Marshal squinted at the screen and picked out images of a dragon, angel, scimitar and Arabic script – no doubt a schlock quotation from the Koran. Many of the photos were captioned. There were a host of pictures featuring members of the Turkish mafia and fellow Albanian gangsters. Shaking hands and back slapping one another. Marshal noted a couple of photos in particular. They were wide-angled shots, encompassing members of the krye's crew. He recognised Bisha and Bashkim. They were referenced as being low-level dealers and enforcers in the organisation. And so, Marshal had attacked a couple of minnows on the food chain. But he was willing to work his way up to the big fish. A number of photos of Rugova's mistresses were also included in the documents. The Albanian may not have had the best taste in clothes, but Marshal couldn't fault his taste in women. As much as there may have been an air of swagger and menace in the krye's expression, Marshal couldn't deny the joy and devotion in his eyes when pictured with his children. Rugova probably wasn't a complete monster. But he was a monster, nevertheless. One who needed slaying.

Despite the dry and officious tone of many of the reports, a sense of frustration and failure seeped through in the prose. Yet at least one of the officers involved in the case appeared dogged and determined to get his man. A DI Martin Elmwood. Marshal made a mental note of his name and saved his contact details to his phone. Elmwood had been the one to authorise a raid on the nightclub. Although the raid had ultimately proved fruitless, Elmwood still believed that the club, registered under

Rugova's name, should still be a focus of their surveillance and investigation. Sooner or later the Albanian would make a mistake. Arms or a significant amount of cocaine would be warehoused there. Or someone would be tortured or murdered at the venue, with the boss present.

Marshal would prove equally dogged and determined, he promised himself. He balled his hand into a fist and felt his heart pumping. But instead of experiencing a sense of rage or fear, Marshal felt a strange sense of liberation or even contentment. Purpose. And it wasn't due to the endorphins released in his system from his run. Marshal realised that he no longer felt bored – and boredom was so often the enemy of a soldier.

Marshal couldn't be bothered to correct people at the time, but friends and family thought he originally enlisted in the army to please his father. But Marshal enrolled at Sandhurst in order to prove something to the world, or rather to himself. The army would help him fight off the despair and melancholy he suffered from. Fuelled by pride and ego, he wanted to be a man apart. 3 Para would also be a stepping stone to reach his goal of 22 SAS. That was the plan. But man plans, God laughs. Thankfully, he no longer had any regrets about failing to reach the Regiment. The SAS could manage without him. The bullet in his shoulder had nearly killed him. But, ironically, it may have also saved him. The ultimate goal could have proved a gaol. Enlisting in the army had been one of the best decisions he had ever made. But leaving it had been another.

His eyes grew tired and he pinched the bridge of his nose. There was still a wealth of intelligence to plough through. But he needed some fresh air – and some coffee.

Bars of sunlight slanted through the bedroom window, between the curtains. Porter's head remained resolutely relaxed, sunk into his goose-feather pillow. He slept in, along with his wife. The children were staying with friends. They could indulge themselves. The husband had briefly woken earlier to bring some freshly squeezed orange juice and a warmed-up croissant to his wife. Breakfast in bed. It was the least he could do, to repay the supper he devoured after getting home last night. Even though he had eaten lamb cutlets at the club, Porter – inspired by love and his wife's cooking – managed to eat a second meal.

Victoria gently rubbed her silken leg against her husband's shin. He smelled her skin and hair, breathing in the scent like a favourite perfume.

"I should get up," Victoria said, yawning and stretching out her elegant figure.

"No, you shouldn't. We should have some more "us" time. I should really be sweeping you off your feet and taking you on a romantic weekend to Vienna or Lisbon. We could leave the children to fend for themselves. But I'm mean. I like the discount they provide us with, from a group booking," Porter drily remarked. He was intending, however, to arrange a trip for just him and his wife soon. The plan would be to arrange a fortnight stay at a luxury resort. Follow the sun. The only small problem was organising for someone to take care of Violet. He would rather book a holiday with the Khmer Rouge than leave her in a kennel or with strangers.

Victoria smiled and rolled her eyes. She had grown accustomed to her husband's dry sense of humour. Needs must.

"I need to get up. I've a few things to sort before Grace arrives this afternoon. What time are you expecting your driver? James, isn't it? We can trust him, can't we? I don't want him leering at Grace or trying to hit on her."

"He'll be fine. He's a former officer, no less. Not just some Tom," Porter replied. His wife was from a military family and she was aware that "Tom" was a shortening of "Tomcat", a nickname for paratroopers. Forever on the prowl.

"It's the officers you need to watch out for more," Victoria countered, knowing all too well how officers liked to think they were God's gift to women. More than one officer had made a play for her over the years, even when she had subtly mentioned she was a married woman. Or especially when she had mentioned she was married. Grace had recently complained to her aunt, over the phone, how she was tired of photographers, casting agents and actors hitting on her, expecting them to fall for their looks or charms. Victoria didn't want her niece adding "soldier" to the list of professions.

Porter recalled how, the night before, he had asked Marshal to give his word of honour, that he would treat the model as a client, as opposed to would-be conquest.

"And I hope "honour" isn't just a mere word for you."

"Mine honour is my life; both grow in one. Take honour from me, and my life is done," Marshal replied, quoting Shakespeare, whilst finishing off the Claret.

Even the devil can quote Shakespeare for his own purposes, Porter thought, whilst catching the waiter's eye to order another bottle. Usually, he was adept at reading people (he sometimes knew them better than they knew themselves), but, annoyingly, Porter couldn't quite tell whether Marshal was being sarcastic or not.

A grey paste of a sky was smeared overhead. The strong breeze caused the fallen leaves to rustle together and swirl-up. They slapped against brickwork, cars and his shins. A train rumbled over the nearby railway bridge. An overweight toddler wailed, almost stripping the paint from the walls. His overweight mum, wearing god-awful pyjama bottoms, wheeled the piglet past. Marshal regretted not bringing out his headphones, not that he would be able to turn down the volume on some of the outfits he encountered.

Marshal made his way, across the Walworth Road, towards *Hej Coffee*. During his ten-minute walk, he received a couple of messages from Alison. The first was still laced with scorn and righteous indignation. The second contained an olive branch. She wanted to meet and understand what happened. If it was possible to remain friends. She even ended the message with an "x".

Frailty thy name is woman.

Marshal thought it best not to reply to either text. He did reply to Porter, however, when he asked what time he would reach his house later. Marshal intended to set-off around 14.00 to avoid the rush hour, although the traffic would be snarled up around Hammersmith no matter what. He just needed to pack a bag when he got back home. He wondered which books he should take with him. It was likely that his days, driving her from meeting to meeting, would involve waiting around a lot. Perhaps the job would grant him a window to finally re-read *The Idiot*. Every cloud has a silver lining.

Hej Coffee. Hej translates as "Hello" in Swedish. If there was a better cup of coffee in London, then Marshal had yet to find it. Sometimes he liked his coffee black, bitter. Sometimes he took it with milk and two sugars. It all depended on his mood. He often stayed for two cups. The first would wake him up, and the second would perk him up.

He smoked a couple of cigarettes, watching the world go by, on the wooden benches outside, before entering. The coffee shop had its own roastery and Marshal never tired of being greeted by the aroma of freshly roasted beans. The smell was up there with freshly baked bread, petrol, a new hardback book and cordite. The lines of the café's modern interior were softened through comfortable seats and a warm atmosphere. Marshal liked that any and everyone came to the café, not just coffee snobs. Hej was also wonderfully dog-friendly. Marshal preferred the company of Bruno (a bounding staffie cross), Freya (a scampering black spaniel), Oreo (a dog who thought it was a cat) and Coco (a fantastically miserable sausage dog) to any coffee snob. Or socialist.

Marshal popped in on most days and was a familiar face to staff and customers alike. He offered up a smile and nod of greeting to a few regular patrons. Jeff Barnacle lowered the copy of *The Daily Telegraph* he was reading and said hello. Jeff was comfortably the best-dressed person at the coffee shop. He was also the most comfortably right-wing. Sitting on a table next to Jeff was the avuncular James Galpot. James had played guitar with Clapton and Hendrix in the sixties, and still had a twinkle in his eye and an ear for a good blues riff. The Para offered a respectful and fraternal nod to Iain Dalton too - or rather Captain Iain Dalton, who was on leave. Marshal may have lost confidence in the political class in the country, but, if the likes of Iain were anything to go by, the officer class in the army still had something about it.

Marshal also said "Hello" (he refused to say "Hej") to Matt, one of the co-owners of the café, who was training some staff in the roastery.

The Kiwi's knowledge and enthusiasm for his product was infectious. Matt called himself the biggest "drug dealer in South London", what with the amount of caffeine he peddled. He loved the sound of the roaster churning out the beans. It was his second favourite sound in the world, behind that of the tills ringing.

Marshal sat down with his black coffee, at his usual table, with his back to the wall, and opened his laptop.

Viktor Baruti.

Throughout the files so far Baruti had been referred to as a *"kryetar… head of operations… chief intelligence officer… chief counter-intelligence officer… chief enforcer… assassin."*

Marshal was intrigued, not least because the Albanian was born two days after his own date of birth. He was a gifted student, his region's fencing champion as a teenager and a sniper in the army. Baruti was proficient in *Krav Maga* and spoke five languages. He was unmarried and untattooed. For some Albanian gangsters, taking their cue from their Russian counterparts, their ink told the stories of their life (and crimes). Yet it seems that Baruti had no interest in being an open book, for others to read. The kryetar was well-conditioned. Glossy black hair hung down over a smooth brow. From the photos included in the files, Baruti owned a gamut of facial expressions, from brooding to glowering. He needed to smile more, in the face of such a bleak world, Marshal fancied. The muscles, located in the corner of his mouth, were probably the only ones he didn't exercise. His hands were bony and strong, and Marshal envisioned them gripping a gun or knife like a talon. His eyes were an icy blue, his nose sharp, like a blade.

Baruti was already purported to be responsible for multiple hits in his native country, but the bulk of the intelligence on the Albanian naturally focussed on the crimes committed in

Glasgow and London. His first murder in Scotland was, arguably, as a result of self-defence. The attack occurred within a month of the Albanians operating in the city. A couple of drug dealers, from Anderston, confronted Baruti one night. The Scots, carrying baseball bats, cornered their competitor, who had been dealing on their turf. Their intention was to break a few bones. Send a message. But it was the Albanian who sent out a message. The Scots were found dead, in the street. Fingers had been cut off. Ears severed. Eyes gouged out.

The gruesome murders were a taste of things to come. Baruti was always careful not to leave any hard evidence at the scene of a crime – and no one would ever testify against the Albanian – but the police were left in little doubt as to who was responsible. Marshal remained impassive, just about, and continued to sip his coffee as he read over the files.

Jimmy Macall, who was never without an entourage, considered himself "untouchable". But Baruti killed him with a shot from a sniper's rifle, from a roof, 250 yards away. The bullet struck him in the chest. The report noted that it was a windy day. Marshal would have been proud of the shot himself.

Baruti was also suspected of torturing and murdering Mohammed Faris, a kebab shop owner and dealer who was part of the gang's distribution network. The police believed that Faris was skimming. After burning his face on the grill and inserting kebab skewers into his palms and genitals Baruti injected heroin directly into his brain and Faris died from an overdose.

In terms of a more conventional hit, Marshal read a report about the enforcer walking to into a bar, just off the Paisley Road, and shooting a local crime boss. Two taps to the chest and then one to the head. Baruti must have scouted the scene first, as he managed to avoid the CCTV cameras, both inside and outside the venue.

He had already made his mark in London too, in retaliation to the West Indian gang, led by Delroy Onslow, murdering an Albanian. The gang had left their calling card – that of leaving a Jamaican flag alongside their victim. Baruti entered the yardie's flat. He first cut his face to ribbons with a Stanley knife. He died from asphyxiation, however, as the Albanian stuffed his own country's flag down his victim's throat.

Viktor Baruti was a person of interest to the police, to put things mildly. He knew how to spot and lose a tail – and seemed to carry out his activities regardless of their surveillance. The NCA suspected that the Albanian had bribed or intimidated police personnel, in order to gain counter-intelligence. The gang always seemed prepared when their places of business or recreation were raided. At one point, Elmwood focussed his attention on shutting down one of their brothels in Peckham. Yet, when the raid took place, the brothel had relocated to an unknown location.

Marshal read a file on one Albanian woman, Agnesa, who had escaped from one of the establishments. She approached the police and Elmwood interviewed her. Her story was a tragic, if not an uncommon, one. Agnesa had been sold to the gang in Milot, in payment for her husband's unpaid gambling debts. She was taken to Glasgow and, along with a dozen other women, was imprisoned in a flat above a bar. For six months, she was forced to become a prostitute – and often gang-raped by members of Rugova's crew. Agnesa mentioned that most of the women became addicted to heroin. It kept them docile and dependent, and deadened the misery of their captivity. Yet, more than one of the women committed suicide. When Agnesa's friend, Drita, escaped, Baruti tracked her down and brought her back to the brothel. He stood Drita in front of the other women in the living-room and shot her in the head, threatening that Agnesa and others would suffer the same fate if they tried to flee. It was a testament to her courage that Agnesa still fled, shortly after the incident. She could not be convinced to testify against Baruti, however.

"He will find me. He would also find and murder my family back in Albania too... The devil works in mysterious ways... You should thank me for it. Because he would get to you all as well."

One of the conclusions of Elmwood and the NCA was that to truly disband the organisation, they would need to convict both Rugova and Baruti. If one of them remained, then so would the gang. Their task would prove more difficult because, technically, Baruti could claim diplomatic immunity. One answer was to present the Albanian diplomatic service with so much damning evidence, they would be compelled to revoke his status and send him home.

The half-smile just about clung onto Marshal's expression. He recalled Porter's description of Baruti:

"He's an Albanian Pinkie," he said, taking it for granted that his dinner companion was familiar with *Brighton Rock*, either the film or the book. "He probably even carries a bottle of Vitriol and a cut-throat razor around with him... Wickedness is a real thing in this world. I wish I could say the same for goodness. But somehow goodness slips through our hands, like thin air. But as many lives as our Pinkie has ruined, we should not allow him to spoil our dinner. I may well order some chocolate cake. I need to raise my spirits – and serotonin levels."

Porter forced a smile after he spoke, his face still haunted by the thought of Baruti catching up with Marshal. Later, during the train journey home to Windsor, Porter promised himself that he would help Marshal out in any way he could (although he still told himself he was retired). The ex-Guards officer lost Devlin. He did not want to lose Marshal too.

9.

His eyes grew tired again and his heart grew heavy. Marshal closed the laptop and appreciated the distraction as Jeremy Knight, the other owner of the coffee shop, approached him. Not only was he conscious of shielding the material from his friend, but it would have been bad form to keep glancing at the screen whilst chatting to someone. Jeremy had the ability to smile, in the face of having the world on his shoulders. Always an admirable trait. Jeremy also knew where all the best curry houses were in South London. Which Marshal also appreciated.

"Afternoon, James. Beer?" Jeremy asked, albeit he already knew the answer.

"Why not?" Marshal replied. He felt like he now needed something stronger than coffee. The two men regularly drank together. They were both well practised at holding their liquor and a conversation. "Unfortunately, I can only have one, which, of course, means two. Believe it or not, I've actually got some work to do this afternoon."

"Well, I'll believe it when I see it. Will you not just be busy doing nothing, like usual?" Jeremy remarked, after ordering a couple of drinks with just the slightest movements of his head and eyes. Jeremy knew something of Marshal's situation, in relation to his military career – and inheriting a significant sum of money from his grandfather. Enough to be able to live a life of leisure. "What's the job?"

"I'm doing a friend a favour and chauffeuring a former fashion model around town."

"Lucky you."

"I don't feel that lucky. This isn't my first rodeo, so to speak. I've worked for models and celebrities before. I'll have to muster all my energy – and my store of bullshit for the month – in order to feign interest in her conversation. I may have to take a vat of coffee to go as well, to furnish me with enough caffeine to keep me awake. She'll doubtlessly spend most of her time bitching about other models. What's the definition of a misogynist? A man who hates women as much as women hate each other. I suppose I should be grateful for small mercies. It could be worse. I could have to suffer a male model in the back of the car. Or Bono."

Marshal made his way home after a couple of pints. As he closed in on his neighbourhood his eyes flitted from one side of the street to the other, as if he were a squaddie walking down the Shankill Road, in case the Albanians had already inserted watchers into the area. He was also conscious of keeping an eye out for the silver Subaru, and any other suspicious vehicles, parked outside his building.

At the same time, Marshal's inner eye played out various scenarios. War games. The war may already be over. The Albanians could ignore the incident. But hope for the best, plan for the worst. Marshal developed the seed of an idea, to help bring the criminal network down. The keystones were Rugova and Baruti. Take them out and the rest of the organisation would collapse, like a house of cards. When he reached home, he ordered a few items online. Just in case his plan could come to fruition. Marshal then packed a bag for his trip away. He made sure to include his locked metal box, containing the Glock 21, with magazine and suppressor – as well as his copy of Dostoyevsky's *The Idiot*.

Marshal's car was a black Jaguar. The engine coughed, as if bronchial. The steering was a little stiff, as if arthritic. He didn't keep the car in good order. But maybe it was just all in the mind. But then again, everything may be considered just all in the mind. The vehicle scraped through its last service. He didn't know how many miles the car had left in it. It seemed to sometimes creak like an old rocking chair. It could last another twenty years. It could last another day. Like him.

He drove to a petrol station and ran the Jaguar through the carwash. He took the beer can out of the cupholder and threw away the empty cigarette packets in the passenger's footwell.

He was not overly worried about making a good impression. But he didn't want to make a bad one.

He started to listen to the news during his journey through London, but things were all too predictable and partisan. The syrupy or blustering voices of politicians, speaking in sentences a hundred and forty characters long, grated on his threadbare soul. Perhaps the producer of the programme was trying to cultivate the idea of having two opposing people – who would posit a thesis and antithesis. A synthesis, solution, might then be reached. But the outcome was that Marshal just switched off and listened to Bruce Springsteen.

"Hold tight to your anger, and don't fall to your fears…
Bring on your wrecking ball."

Marshal opened the windows to help air the interior. He thought he could still smell his grandfather's scent and cigars. But maybe it was all in his mind again. He frequently drove Edward "Teddy" Marshal to his check-ups and tests at the hospital. His grandfather would sit in the back, as quiet as a mouse – vacant. Or he would rail against the "plastic" and "honourless" world, spittle hitting the back of the headrest. Although his voice became a hoarse whisper towards the end. The years of bellowing out orders, or a lifetime of drinking whisky, caught up with him.

Teddy Marshal served in the SAS during the Second World War. An officer once described the Regiment as "the sweepings of the public schools and the prisons." Teddy had spent time in both. He looked a little bit like Gregory Peck when in his prime, his grandson thought (although towards the end he resembled Scrooge more: white hair, ghostly pale, haunted face). He had a strong jaw and solid frame before that. A sometimes dark, sometimes noble, expression lined his features. After the war, Teddy Marshal set up a successful engineering company. He died, aged ninety-four. His wife, Dorothy, passed away a decade before him. After her passing, something died in Teddy too. He would often call out his wife's name, whether wide awake or asleep. When his grandfather suffered a stroke, his grandson moved-in to take care of him. His rehabilitation went well, he regained his speech and mobility, but at the same time dementia started to eat away at the old man's mind, like rust eating away an at old park bench. His moods became increasingly erratic. He could be forgetful one moment, angry the next. Yet the soldier fought a good fight and tried to retain his sense of humour and decency. His grandson helped alleviate the confusion, loneliness and isolation. But not all of it.

Marshal's half-smile teetered on disappearing, or widening, as he remembered his time with his grandfather. He would shave him every other morning, watch Westerns with him during the afternoon and cook for him in the evening. He would administer his pills, from a dosette box the size of a briefcase, three times a day. He would take him to the park and local café. Teddy Marshal could be irascible and bigoted. He was as stubborn as a Yorkshireman, and although he was devoted to his wife, he wasn't always faithful. But he was kind, courageous – and his black sense of humour lit up most rooms. Like Churchill, he had taken more out of alcohol than alcohol had taken out of him. The veteran was also an unashamed patriot. "If you cut me, I'll bleed red, white and blue." Queen and country meant something. His grandson envied and admired his belief in something bigger than him. "To be born English is to win first prize in the lottery of life," he would say, quoting Cecil Rhodes. Still, his grandson, studying philosophy at the time, remained sceptical. But he realised cynicism could be a double-edged sword, hurting both the person the weapon was pointed towards, and its wielder.

For many years Teddy Marshal remained reticent, in relation to talking about what he did during the war. "I survived, so it was mission accomplished," he remarked to his teenaged grandson. But shortly after moving in to take care of the old soldier, Teddy Marshal began to open up. Perhaps he wanted to exercise his memory more, like a muscle, to help combat the dementia. Or it was the case that although the present was often a blur, the past was as vivid as a photograph. As James Marshal drove the Jaguar westwards, he heard the ghost of his grandfather entertaining and educating him from the backseat.

"Monty's beret was never big enough to fit his enormous head. The diva acted as if he was Eisenhower's superior. He had plenty of dress sense. But as the war went on, he increasingly lacked common sense. Arnhem was a charnel house, a fool's errand. Bill Slim was twice the commander he was. I never heard a single word said against Slim, from the soldiers who served under him... Paddy Mayne. Now there was a giant of a man, in more ways than one. He could be a smart bastard. A bloody-minded bastard. A drunk bastard. But always some sort of bastard. I stayed up drinking with him a few times. He would often say how he wanted to be a poet. But he knew he made a better killer... God, I was scared before any prospective firefight. The drink and Benzedrine probably added an edge, rather than took one away. But it's good to be scared. It means you're human. Yet fear can be overcome, like an enemy... You've never asked me, James, if ever I killed someone during the war. Perhaps because you already know the answer..."

A rare tear welled in his eye as Marshal remembered his grandfather. He was invited to re-take the SAS selection while he looked after him. Marshal could have also worked for Porter during that time – and earned a small fortune. He could have met someone, married and had children. Instead, he resembled Sisyphus each day. Instead, he watched, all but helplessly, as someone he loved dearly deteriorated and died. Yet Marshal had no regrets.

Looking after his grandfather had been one of the saddest things he had ever done, and the most rewarding.

Marshal made good time, getting to his destination. The house was tucked away, close to an affluent, old-fashioned village. The handsome property was surrounded by a high brick wall, and further concealed by strategically placed fruit trees. He parked next to a mud-splattered Range Rover and gleaming Mercedes. Crime pays, Marshal thought to himself.

He was soon greeted by Porter, his wife and a mongrel on the gravel driveway. Violet seemed particularly pleased to see the stranger. Her tail spun around, as opposed to just wagging, and she affectionately licked his hands and jumped up at him.

Marshal's half-smile turned into a fulsome grin. Dogs are happiness machines.

"She likes you," Victoria remarked, on witnessing Violet roll over to let Marshal rub her stomach. She had never known the creature to let a stranger stroke her tummy so quickly.

"I'm sure she will change her mind once she gets to know me," he replied. If Violet had been human, however, the statement would have proved more realistic and less humorous, he imagined.

Viktor Baruti stirred his coffee four times and tapped his spoon twice against the side of the cup, as he sat, alone, in a booth at *The High Life*. He flicked his hair out of his eyes and put the empty glasses on the table back onto their coasters. Baruti had just finished speaking with Bisha and Bashkim again, about the incident. They were too witless, or scared, to dissemble. Despite the kryetar's pointed questions, he was still none the wiser as to whether the Englishman was a random stranger, or a contractor working for one of their rivals. The only way to uncover the truth was to locate and confront him.

"Find him," he instructed, without equivocation. The implication being that if they did not find him, Baruti would find them. Their orders were to patrol the streets in the neighbourhood, using a different vehicle, with the intention of spotting the Englishman. "You are not to engage with the stranger, however. Just follow him and contact me. I will deal with him. I will be able to track your location on my phone."

Profits and pride meant that the Albanians couldn't allow the attack to go unpunished. They would still establish themselves in the area and push their product. Baruti also couldn't allow the Englishman to turn into too much of a distraction. The West Indians were a greater concern. Recent information suggested that Delroy Onslow was recruiting more men. Baruti had obtained a list of the gang's safehouses, and the home addresses of key gang members. If Onslow went on the offensive the kryetar would put them all to the sword. A Night of Long Knives would prove less bloody, and more efficient, than a drawn-out war. The Russians and Chinese would permit the action. They were perhaps even more racist than Albanians, Baruti thought. *Perhaps.*

He glanced at his watch – a gold *Audemars Piguet* – and pursed his lips on noticing a tiny scratch on the glass. He would contact the vendor but, should he be without the timepiece for more than two days in order to replace the glass, he would just buy another. He would feel somehow incomplete without a watch. Nearly as much as he would feel incomplete without his gun.

Baruti would get home later and spend the evening cleaning the *La Marzocco*. Before that, however, he needed to pay a visit to one of his operatives, Valon Hasi. The enforcer had recently posted a video on YouTube of himself and other gang members, brandishing a Kalashnikov and snorting cocaine through fifty-pound notes. Faces and number plates had been blurred out, but it was still an act of stupidity. *Clowns.* Baruti would order Hasi to take the video down, otherwise the next video posted up would involve his torture and death. The former bricklayer, from Fier, thought he was a big man. He was too flash. Too loud. Hasi had a diamond stud in one of his teeth and owned specially designed gold-plated knuckle-dusters. The oaf focussed too much on what was between his legs, rather than what was between his ears. Baruti would cut him down to size if he put the security of their organisation in jeopardy again.

Laughter rang out from a couple of staff members in the nearby kitchens. Baruti pursed his lips even more. The sound grated on the black hole of where his soul used to be.

10.

After being invited into the main house for a cup of coffee, Porter showed Marshal to his billet, a converted "posh shed" in the garden. The guesthouse contained a toilet/shower, as well as a small fireplace, double bed, fridge and television. The Wi-Fi coverage was excellent and Marshal continued to read and re-read the intelligence files. He marvelled at how Porter's contact, Mariner, could have collated so much material, so quickly. Marshal also devoted a little research time to Grace Wilde. She was often called an "English rose" in profile pieces. Her breakthrough in the industry had come when she was seventeen. She had worked with most major designers and fashion houses. Most of the articles mentioned her love life. She had never been married, but had dated a string of actors, sports stars and other miscellaneous celebrities and millionaires. She pouted a lot in photos – appearing doe-eyed, as if she were about to ask someone to buy her a pony. The veteran model had recently announced her retirement.

"I want to settle back in England and take stock... I have been fortunate to earn a good living over the years. It's time to give someone back."

Marshal raised an eyebrow, in scepticism or cynicism. Maybe both. He'd heard such trite before, all too often. The fashion industry had probably moved on, deeming Grace Wilde to be too old for its target demographic. She was pushed, before she jumped, he judged. And now the model was moving on too. Grace Wilde, the brand and company, would probably give enough back to qualify for tax breaks.

Porter mentioned to Marshal to come over for drinks, before dinner, at six o'clock. As he walked across the lawn and driveway, he inadvertently joined the welcome party to greet the guest of honour.

Grace Wilde pulled up in the taxi, which she had booked at the airport. Porter grabbed her bags, as he didn't want his other guest to feel too much like staff.

The evening was drawing in. A crescent moon hung lazily in the sky. Marshal could now view the stars. The constellations fanned themselves across the firmament, like a peacock showing off its feathers. The lamps came on at the front of the house, cutting triangles of light across the drive. Violet scampered towards her new friend. Marshal bent down and stroked the mongrel behind her ear, as she licked his face.

Marshal had pictured the model turning up in *Zanotti* heels, wearing a designer dress costing as much as a small car, with her hair pinned up in an edifice akin to some ghastly modern sculpture. Yet Grace was just wearing some faded jeans, white pumps and a purple lambswool top. Her shoulder-length blonde hair hung down naturally. Marshal noticed she was wearing a thin gold necklace, although the pendant was tucked under her clothes. He imagined that a large diamond was attached to the chain, similar to the one she had worn in a Bulgari photoshoot, which Marshal had seen online.

He conceded that the model was undeniably attractive. It was likely she was undeniably vain too, which would not have made her beautiful, in his eyes. Grace had an oval face, almond-shaped eyes and high cheekbones. She looked like Anne Hathaway. Her blue eyes almost shimmered as much as the stars. Her figure her been willowy during her career, but she had put on a little weight in her retirement. Now she was slender, lithe – and she looked better for it. She moved with an undeniable elegance, although Marshal couldn't quite tell if her elegance was natural, or if it had been drilled into her. He generously leaned towards the former, given her aunt possessed a similar figure and poise.

Victoria and Grace greeted one another with genuine, heartfelt affection and a long, warm hug – as opposed to just air-kissing each other on the cheek.

Although Victoria had spoken to her niece about her driver, giving her as much information as she could, Grace pretended that she didn't even know his name when they were introduced. She narrowed her almond eyes and took him in. He was handsomer and fitter than she expected. He could have been a low-rent male model, in his youth, she imagined. Grace had met plenty of military types before, on both sides of the Atlantic. All stood ramrod straight. Most were repressed – emotionally scarred by their parents, boarding schools or the army. Some were alcoholics. Most were married, most were unfaithful. Some were chinless wonders. Young, dumb and full of...

"Can I trust him?" Grace had asked her aunt. Victoria was aware how, in the past, drivers and other staff had sold pictures and stories about her niece to the press.

"If Oliver trusts him, I do too."

All she needed from him was just to drive, however. Grace would roll her eyes and sigh if he hit on her. She would then give him a verbal warning if he ignored her signals. Finally, she would ask Oliver to replace the ex-soldier if her driver stepped over the line. She was tired of uninteresting men thinking she would be interested in them, just because they worked out at the gym, drove an expensive car or had other women falling at their feet.

"Nice to meet you," Marshal remarked, flashing an amiable smile.

"Nice to meet you too," Grace replied. Her voice was clear and clean, like glass. Cut glass. Grace had grown up in Essex, but she spoke like she came from Surrey. Her smile was polite but appeared and vanished from her face as quickly as a snake's tongue might dart in and out to taste the air.

Marshal subtly surveyed the dining room, as the party of four had drinks before dinner. Most of the furniture was old-fashioned, antique. Yet a softer, more modern aesthetic – and a woman's touch – added something to the room.

He glanced at the bookshelves. There were plenty of titles, fiction and non-fiction, dedicated to the Byzantines. Marshal was unsurprised at Porter's interest in the conniving empire, which proved a master at playing all sides. There were Folio Society editions of Joseph Conrad, John Buchan and Ian

Fleming, as well as various wine atlases and military history titles. Portraits of Porter's antecedents, wearing dress uniforms and portentous expressions, hung on the walls.

Marshal found it interesting, or rather comical, to see Porter in a domestic environment. The ex-Guards officer who had commanded soldiers, blackmailed MPs and arranged contract killings was a doting and devoted husband. Porter willingly helped strain the vegetables and made the gravy when asked to do so. He also followed Victoria's order, as if she were an RSM, when she asked for him to turn Elgar off and put on Celine Dion.

The conversation was stilted over dinner, like a car engine that was unable to turn over in the frost. There was an invisible, yet tangible, tension or awkwardness around the table. Oliver briefed his wife beforehand on an array of topics not to bring up with Marshal (his time in the army, his mother and father, grandfather and Tony Blair). The fixer was quieter than usual. He was distracted, ruminating on whether Marshal would continue his private war with the Albanians – if he was intending to get his retaliation in first. The best thing would be for Marshal to disappear for a while. Porter thought about calling in a favour from a contact and offering Marshal the use of a villa in the Algarve. He also spared a thought for Devlin – and imagined what he might have said and done in Marshal's position.

No retreat, no surrender.

Victoria would sometimes attempt to bring her niece into the conversation, but she never wholeheartedly embraced the invitation – like a debutant forever turning dances down at a ball. She was courteous, but uninterested, in what anyone had to say. Victoria equally failed in trying to engage Marshal. He was often flippant or deflective. He clearly didn't feel comfortable talking about himself. Ironically, because he could be self-deprecating and elusive Victoria was keen to get to know Marshal more.

After dessert Grace announced that she had to excuse herself. She was tired from her flight and needed to go to bed. Grace mentioned that she and Marshal needed to be up early –

acting like a schoolteacher, reminding a child that he had an exam in the morning.

It was Marshal's turn to roll his eyes. The model was as aloof as a politician's wife. Too important to lower herself to interact with staff, or mere mortals. She probably thought she was some form of classical statue, to be admired rather than touched.

After Grace took her leave, her aunt apologised for her niece.

"I am sorry if she seemed out of sorts. She has had a long journey, what with the flight and all the arrangements to come back to the country."

"It's fine. Certainly, you have nothing to apologise for. Rather I should be thanking you for a delicious meal," Marshal replied. The lamb had fallen off the bone, as easily as civil servants had fallen down in the heat of Helmand. The carrots and broccoli had been crunchy, and the roast potatoes had been crispy on the outside and fluffy inside. For dessert, which he had eaten seconds of, Victoria had cooked a rhubarb crumble. Marshal remembered how his mum also flavoured her crumbles with raisins and cinnamon, as he ate the pudding. He couldn't remember the last time he had sat around a family dinner table and had a meal. The last time had probably been with an ex-girlfriend and her family. The relationship had not likely lasted much longer after such a gathering. But it had been far too long since he had enjoyed such delicious homecooked food.

Usually, Porter would invite a houseguest, particularly a fellow officer, to stay up and have a cognac and cigar with him. They would chat about MOD cuts, mutual acquaintances and how the world was going to hell in a handcart. But he was tired. He also feared Grace's wrath, should he keep her driver up too late and cause him to have a hangover in the morning. Marshal was fine to retire early too, what with having some sleep, cigarettes and reading to catch up on.

Grace offered up a genuine yawn, and two feigned ones, at dinner to convey how exhausted she was. She hoped that

Victoria didn't think her too rude for making it an early night. She wanted to ask after Victoria more, about her children and how Oliver was faring in his retirement, but she felt it inappropriate with a stranger, staff member, in their midst.

Her room upstairs had a bathroom and Grace showered. She then went through her beauty routine and ablutions, before bed. She slumped onto the mattress, in her pearl-coloured silk dressing gown, stretching out her body, uncoiling her anxieties and muscles.

To her slight surprise, she found herself thinking about her driver. Perhaps she had been a tad too curt and standoffish towards him at dinner. But she told herself that it was important to establish a professional relationship and boundaries with him. Violet seemed smitten with him, however. She couldn't quite place his accent and his back wasn't ramrod straight. She didn't know whether to be impressed or worried, that he worked his way through a bottle of wine at the same pace as Oliver. He was wittier than most officers she had ever encountered, and the corner of her mouth flicked upwards, for a second too, as she recalled snippets of his conversation.

"The annoying thing about a near-death experience is that you see your life flash before you. Suffice to say I nearly died of boredom, re-living certain episodes, before any enemy could get to me... I do not set my life at a pin's fee."

Grace's ears pricked-up on hearing the soldier quote Hamlet, although she did her best not to show any interest. She would have considered that the driver was unwittingly quoting Shakespeare, until he quoted the play later in the evening too:

"Nothing is good or bad but thinking makes it so."

Grace yawned again, for real, but still, she worked through a couple more emails on her tablet. She was starting a small business and was conscious that people would soon be relying on her for their livelihoods. It felt good to be doing something different. She breathed in the air when getting off the plane. It wasn't the cleanest air in the world. But it was home. She was free.

For too long the fashion model had lived in a gilded cage. She lived in an apartment overlooking Central Park. She had a personal assistant, branding manager and cleaner. She could secure tickets to whatever she wanted, whenever she wanted. Most of her clothes were given to her. She dated actors and dot.com millionaires, who thought that the size of their bank accounts could compensate them for being morally bankrupt. Most of her dates were arranged through publicists. She ate at the finest restaurants (although she had to severely limit what she could eat), holidayed in the best resorts. Photos of dates were leaked to the press. She was an ornament to most of her boyfriends, to be shown off and displayed like a diamond engagement ring. Everyone said how "fabulous" and "gorgeous" she was, as if a Chorus to her life. Most days were spent reading, going to the gym in her apartment building and attending meetings, photoshoots and fashion shows. Foul, egotistical photographers would hit on her as par for the course. The only ones who didn't were the pederasts. Cocaine was placed on glass coffee tables in front of her, far more than cups of coffee. Friends constantly popped pills and attended therapy, believing that they were tortured and interesting. A gilded cage is still a cage. Grace had begun to hate her life – and herself – in New York. She wanted to turn the page. It was good to be back in England. Back for good. She missed marmalade, the countryside and sarcasm.

Grace finally turned off her tablet and drifted off to sleep, debating to herself whether she preferred Shakespeare or Chekhov.

11.

Marshal, as per the itinerary Grace emailed him with, was waiting in the car at 7.00. There was a chill in the air, not just emanating from his passenger. The former model wore a cream blouse and pencil skirt, which showed off her tanned legs and the svelte lines of her figure. She wore little make-up. Her hair was pinned up. She issued a formal "good morning" and offered up another forced smile, before sitting in the back and immersing herself in her tablet.

She tapped away furiously, as well as took a series of calls. Half her conversations were with estate agents, relating to buying a property in the Chiswick and Turnham Green area of London. Grace was precise, clinical, with her instructions. Her budget was two million. She wanted a garden, and to be in walking distance from the river. She also wanted sufficient room to have two spare bedrooms for guests, and an office. Other calls were devoted to Grace setting-up a business, a shop located in Chiswick. She received one call from a friend.

Grace didn't have time for any small talk with her driver. Or she didn't want to apportion any time for it. Occasionally she sighed, when the car slowed to a crawl, for being caught in traffic. She kept herself to herself, which was fine by Marshal as he did the same. Some clients in the past endlessly talked, or boasted, to the driver about their life. Or they thought that the Jaguar was some kind of confessional. At least there was no danger of the model getting drunk, overeating and being sick in the back of the vehicle. Marshal craved a cigarette but sensed his passenger would complain if he lit up or opened a window. He was mindful of not driving too fast or too slowly. Goldilocks in the back would want things just right, he mused.

The weather was clement. A canary-yellow sun hung in the sky. Wisps of clouds marked a shimmering blue sky. He did his best to tune out the growling traffic and abrasive car horns, full of sound and fury – signifying nothing.

Marshal thought about Delroy Onslow. *The enemy of my enemy is my friend.* The West Indian gangster had come over from Jamaica in his teens. He wasn't quite the Windrush generation. Onslow had been in and out of prison in his twenties, for various drug and violent offences. For the past ten years, however, Onslow had got smart, and rich, off the back of the capital's appetite for weed and cocaine. He brought over an army of personnel from Jamaica. He was also rumoured to have recruited a number of small youth gangs in South London, who distributed product and attacked rival teen gangs. He owned a nightclub in New Cross, *The Rum Punch*, as well as a West Indian bakery. Onslow was on the backfoot, in relation to his turf war with the Albanians. He could be desperate rather than defeated. He could use an ally, although Marshal wondered if he could trust the gangster. Similarly, why should Onslow trust him? He could well suffer a beating, or worse, if he just walked into the Jamaican's club and presented himself to the psychotic crime boss. Marshal also didn't want his ears assaulted by the grime and drill music they reportedly played at *The Rum Punch*.

Whilst gridlocked in traffic outside of Hammersmith, Marshal tracked his recent online purchases. They were due to arrive tomorrow. He had arranged for his neighbour to accept the parcels for him.

Marshal's first stop was at the estate agents, *Biddingtons*, on Chiswick High St. Grace asked Marshal to wait in the car. The large glass front of the outlet meant that Marshal could observe the whole office leap up from their chairs to greet the minor celebrity (and client, looking to spend two million pounds on a property). From their body language alone, he could discern their attitudes. Some leered. Some fawned, wringing their hands and bowing their heads slightly. A couple of attractive women offered the model a less welcoming expression, when Grace's back was turned. Marshal found their reactions amusing and contemptible in equal measure.

He welcomed the break and smoked a couple of cigarettes in a row, before heading across the road to grab a coffee. Marshal shunned the chains to pop into an independent shop. The morning rush had ended. A father, with his toddler son, sat in the corner. A couple of postmen stood waiting for their order, either winding down from a shift or gearing up for one. Marshal asked for a black coffee and then headed to the facilities at the back of the establishment.

He entered the white-tiled toilets. There were two cubicles and three urinals. There were also two youths – one black, one white – by the sinks, bending over and doing a line of cocaine. Marshal sighed. His shoulders slumped and he rolled his eyes. Disappointment eclipsed anger. He wondered if he went looking for trouble, or trouble found him. The black twenty-year-old, Trevor (he gave himself the more glamorous nickname of "MC Razor"), had the taut, wiry build of a welterweight. A logo, which Marshal didn't recognise, had been shaven into his head. He was wearing a black tracksuit, high-top trainers and a baseball cap (back to front, of course). He was dressed like a Scouser, which was crime enough for Marshal. His pasty friend next to him, Nigel, was wearing Lycra cycling shorts and a waterproof jacket, with a "Radiohead" concert t-shirt underneath. A trendy record bag and *Giro* cycling helmet lay at his feet. Marshal suspected that the gangly, lank-haired adolescent was a bicycle courier, student or, God help him, he worked in the media. His cheeks were hollowed out. A small earring hung out of his left cheek. He appeared half spaced-out and stared at Marshal as if he was trying to bring him into focus.

"Fuck off, or I'll cut ya," Trevor warned, his eyes bloodshot. Wired. The plumber's son from Ealing put on his best patois accent.

"You haven't seen nothing," Nigel added, slightly slurring his words.

Marshal wasn't quite sure what irritated him more, the insult, threat or use of the double negative. He thought how the likes of Luka Rugova only existed because of the likes of the two specimens in front of him. He pictured the scene of the father and son outside walking in on the pair – and being threatened and suffering abuse. Somehow the possible bike courier represented every self-righteous, fascistic cyclist who ever jumped a red light or wore a *GoPro* camera.

"Drugs can be bad for your health," Marshal drily advised. He would have found it difficult to remove the mocking tone from his voice, even if he tried to.

Trevor walked, or rather strutted, over to the stranger. The drugs emboldened the youth to front up to Marshal. He could smell weed on his breath.

Nigel nervously sniggered. He wanted his friend to shame and humiliate the straight-laced guy in the suit, to send him packing so he could do another line.

"I can be bad for your fucking health, bruv," the drug dealer exclaimed, as he started to suck air through his teeth. He was angry at the stranger for disturbing them. He was just about to convince his regular customer to buy what he called a "bargain bucket". Five grams of coke for £200. Before he could finish sucking air through his teeth and make a dismissive kissing sound, however, Marshal delivered a brutal haymaker and floored the youth, like a middleweight knocking out a welterweight. The ex-Para, who had experienced plenty of bouts of milling over the years, knew how to direct a powerful punch without injuring his own hand. The sound of the stranger's fist crunching against the cartilage in his friend's nose made Nigel's stomach turn.

He wasn't sniggering any more, but gulping, as Marshal approached and came into focus. His muscles twitched around his mouth and he let out a whimper. Marshal glanced at the aluminium foil, razor blade and remnants of a line of cocaine on the sink top. The sight disgusted and angered him. He also noticed an enamel badge on the cyclist's jacket, *"Jeremy Corbyn is Our Saviour,"* as he grabbed the druggie by the throat, as if he were a scrawny-necked chicken, and shoved him against the wall. Nigel's bladder gave way a little. His face was contorted in dread, whilst Marshal's expression remained almost equitable, as the soldier covered the youth's mouth with one hand and pulled the earring out of his cheek with the other. Despite muffling the scream, the snivelling was still audible. The small tearing sound of the skin was succeeded by a jet of blood spitting across the toilet and marking the white-tiled floor.

"I did warn you that drugs can be bad for your health," Marshal remarked, before dropping the earring in the sink and walking out the room.

Marshal understandably ordered his coffee to go. He left a healthy tip for the barista, hoping the small courtesy would balance out the account for his venial sins in the toilet. He bought a couple of burner phones on the high street, headed back to the car and read a few chapters of Dostoyevsky, whilst waiting for Grace to return.

Marshal's half-smile was made of stern stuff, and it still lined his features, despite his altercation at the coffee shop, and despite being greeted by Grace's serious, if not stern, expression as she got in the car.

"How did your meeting go?"

"I think that every fifth word which came out of the estate agent's mouth may have had a semblance of truth about it." Grace replied. After being clear that she had a ceiling of two million to spend, she was exasperated to find that the cheapest property they suggested cost two and a half million. "I imagine that's quite a high ratio in their profession."

For once a quirky, wry half-smile broke out on the model's face. Perhaps she did have a sense of humour, as well as a sense of style, Marshal considered.

"One in five? You may well be dealing with the most honest estate agents in the capital then. With integrity like that, they could qualify to work as a Treasury official or BBC news editor."

"I'm not sure if it's refreshing, or tiresome, that some things in London never change. Lies come as easily to some people as breathing. Tamara, from the agency, said she will be out in a minute or two – which probably means over five minutes – to show us to the first property," Grace said. As she finished speaking, she noticed the paperback on the dashboard, her eyes narrowing to discern the title of the book. Her half-smile increased, and she gazed at Marshal with a sense of curiosity, instead of indifference, for once.

"What are you reading?"

"Dostoyevsky. *The Idiot*. It's heartening to know that there was once someone on the planet as depressed as I am," Marshal said, drolly. Grace couldn't quite tell if he was being serious or not.

"I remember reading the book, many years ago. I went through a Russian phase. Tolstoy, Pushkin, Chekhov. It was all food for thought. It's the only kind of food an agent allows a fashion model to eat," Grace half-joked. "Not only did I love to read when waiting around on shoots – and there was plenty of waiting around – but fewer people disturb you when you appear engrossed in a book."

"I have outlived my aspirations,
I have outloved my every dream,
Suffering is my sole persuasion,
My heart feels only what has been.

Green was my garland – it has faded,
Blown by a destiny severe,
But I live on, alone and jaded,
Wondering if my end is near.

Defeated by the autumn frost,
With winter whistling down the heath,
On a bare branch, alone and lost,
I'm a forgotten, shivering leaf.

Pushkin. I read quite a bit whilst waiting around as a soldier."

Grace appeared astounded, if not mesmerised, by Marshal's recital of the poem, impressed by his memory and performance. Her mouth was agape, forming a small circle, as if she were about to be kissed. Her skin tingled. His words and melancholy voice resonated, like music. Grace was used to men who could only quote Donald Trump's tweets, or Drake lyrics.

"I'm not sure I've ever met a chauffeur before, who could quote Pushkin."

"And I've never met a model who has read Tolstoy. It's a novel experience."

"Is that a bad pun?"

"No, I think it's a terrible one. I apologise," Marshal said, with a lop-sided grin.

Grace noticed how Marshal usually had a half-amused, or bemused, expression on his face, as if he were sharing a private joke with himself. She liked how he had the ability to laugh at the world – and himself.

"I should apologise too. I behaved pretty awfully last night, at dinner. I was far from at my best."

"You were tired."

"No, I was terrible. I need to get out of the professional habit of acting like a bitch. It's almost a clause in the contract for being a model. In New York, if you don't treat someone like shit then they'll treat you like shit. It's the law of the urban jungle. But it's no excuse. Not that it's going to wholly make it up to you, but feel free to smoke. You will be fine to open the window. It's about time I had a bad hair day. It's probably been fifteen years since the last one. You can play some music too. Just so long as it isn't trance music or jazz. Or Bono. Also, I would love it if you could attend a meeting with me this afternoon. I'd welcome your opinion on a few issues. I'll go through things when we get there, if that's okay?"

For the first time in a long time, Marshal was curious and intrigued. What was the meeting? What advice did she want?

"Just so long as you know beforehand that my opinion will probably be ill-informed and underwhelming."

"With qualifications like that, you could well get a job as a Treasury official or estate agent."

Marshal grinned again. They both did. During the rest of the day, he would infrequently look in his rear-view mirror and snatch clandestine glances at his passenger. His features remained impassive, masking the fact that Grace was beginning to impress him. She sometimes appeared pensive, or wistful. They were not the expressions he usually associated with fashion models, he somewhat uncharitably thought. Like

Grace Wilde, James Marshal was not immune to pride and prejudice.

12.

Tamara, a thirty-year-old platinum blonde wearing a short skirt, silk-like suit jacket and cherry-red blouse, came out ten minutes later. Her heels clicked on the pavement, her perfume scented the air more than Marshal's cigarette smoke. She was pretty, busty, fake-tanned. Either consciously or consciously, she walked like Barbara Windsor – her hips pneumatically powering the rest of her body. Her eyelashes were false, and Tamara had expertly applied lipstick to make her mouth seem fuller, riper. She smiled broadly, winningly, and Marshal imagined that she had worked as an air stewardess in a previous life. Tamara greeted the driver with a sunnier attitude to that of her client, eyeing up Marshal like a new property that had come onto the market.

"If you would like to follow me. It's only a short drive to the first viewing. If you get lost, just call me," Tamara brightly remarked, handing her card to the attractive chauffeur. She liked the way his body filled out his suit. His car was reasonably expensive. But his watch was very expensive, she noted. No wedding ring either. Not that it would much matter.

"Thanks, Tamara," Marshal replied, flashing a smile which was bright and friendly too.

"Ciao for now," the estate agent said, fluttering her elongated eyelashes, before using her well-oiled hips to walk to her white Audi TT, two cars down.

Grace refrained from taking out her tablet during the drive. Perhaps she thought the journey would be short. Or perhaps she didn't wish to be rude – and wanted to chat to Marshal more. She asked him a few questions. Where did he live in London? When did he first meet Oliver? Marshal duly took an interest in Grace in return. How long had she lived in New York for? What did she miss most about being away from England?

The conversation flowed, with the ease of a babbling brook. They made each other laugh, more than once. Grace thought him smart, self-effacing. He was attractive, without being vain. Confident without being arrogant. When Grace laughed or cracked a joke Marshal noticed how her refined accent slipped a little and the girl from Southend could be glimpsed behind the couture model. But he liked that.

Marshal waited in the car again as they arrived at the townhouse on Airedale Avenue and Tamara showed Grace the property. He tried to read but found himself distracted. Not by Albanian gangsters. But by Grace. When he first met "the English rose" the previous evening Marshal had judged her as being thorny. But he had been wrong. Or at best only half-right. She had a softer, wittier, wiser side, he realised. Not many fashion models, let alone people he knew, had read *War & Peace* and could quote Milton.

Tamara appeared from out of the house on her own. She sashayed up to his car. Marshal already had the window down. He couldn't be sure, but he thought that she had undone another button on her blouse since their first encounter. She bent down, her head nearly poking through the window, as she spoke. He breathed in her perfume, as if taking a drag on a cigarette.

"I hope I didn't drive too quickly for you earlier."

"No, it was fine. I'm used to fast women," Marshal replied, playfully. He may have given his word of honour not to flirt with Grace, but he had made no such commitment relating to the rest of womankind.

Tamara let out a laugh, before tucking a few strands of hair behind her ears.

"Where's Grace?"

"She just wanted to take a further look around the kitchen and garden. She said she would be no longer than five minutes. She's really nice."

"Yes, she is," Marshal said, with more conviction than he would have replied with an hour ago.

"She mentioned that you used to be in the army."

Marshal briefly tried to work out whether Grace had been speaking about him, or if Tamara had asked after him.

"Yes, for my sins."

"How long were you in the army for?"

"Long enough to make a killing."

The blonde estate agent paused to process the comment before laughing again, witnessing the smirk on the driver's face.

"You're funny," Tamara remarked, or almost chirped, before lightly placing her hand on the driver's muscular forearm, which rested on the window. The estate agent probably flirted so much, in both her professional and personal life, that she wasn't always aware she was doing it, Marshal fancied. Tamara had already conducted two affairs with senior colleagues in the office. Junior colleagues had made a play for her, but she preferred men to boys. They had more experience, and money. According to her online profiles Tamara liked shopping, sushi and keeping fit. Her dream, when younger, had been to marry a Premiership footballer. Unfortunately, she only got as far as sleeping with a squad player from one of the lower divisions. She was currently dating a tax lawyer, but it was nothing serious. She had never been out with a soldier before. It might be fun.

Marshal recognised certain indicators of interest and was tempted to ask the estate agent out. A part of him was attracted to her. He knew which part. But he also knew he didn't have time for another meaningless relationship. He needed to focus on the Albanians. But he would keep her card.

Another burst of braying laughter filled the air – and Tamara placed her hand on the driver's forearm again – as Grace came out of the house. She found the sound of her laughter annoying, unprofessional. She didn't stop to consider that her pang of irritation may have been a pang of jealousy.

They were quickly on the road again, heading to the next property. Grace had a schedule to keep and she was keen not to just let the estate agent linger and idly chat to her chauffeur. The model understood that flirting may be part of her job, but there was no need to work overtime.

"She seems to like you," Grace casually mentioned, angling for Marshal's thoughts and intentions. But he wasn't biting.

"She'll like the commission from any sale even more," he replied, deflecting, before asking Grace what she thought of the property.

"It was good, but not great. Do you like where you live?"

"There are worse places to live, although the area still needs cleaning up a bit. I have a nice roof terrace, however. I often go up there to work my way through a book or a couple of beers with my neighbour."

The next viewing was a penthouse at a swanky new apartment building. The views from the large balcony were described as "desirable". The complex housed its own gym and coffee shop. The interior was modern. Too modern. Ideally, Grace wanted a garden – and a dog. Neither of which the property could facilitate. She couldn't help but notice how most of the residents didn't have any curtains or blinds across their windows. Perhaps they were part of the Instagram generation – and happy for their lives to be an open book (but one not worth reading). Or the residents were keen to flaunt their taste and material possessions. One of the residents, surreptitiously or not, stepped out onto his decking in his Birkenstocks, on seeing Grace on the balcony opposite. His unblinking, unwavering gaze made her skin crawl. She later joked to Marshal that he looked like a sex offender. She just couldn't tell whether he was registered or not. He laughed. He loved a good paedophile joke, it separated the sheep from the goats in terms of people having a healthy sense of humour. It was also a gift that kept on giving for those who rushed to act offended.

Again, Tamara was happy to give Grace some time and space to view the property in private, as she ventured downstairs to chat to Marshal.

The chauffeur grasped the opportunity to stretch his legs and smoke a cigarette during the viewing. He also swapped a few text messages with Porter. Victoria wanted to take her niece out to dinner this evening, in order to catch up with her properly. Porter was tasked with looking after the dog. He would cook a meal and share a bottle of whisky with Marshal.

Grace pursed her lips more firmly and her scowl was more pronounced as she observed Tamara enjoying the company of her driver. She spoke curtly to the agent, asserting that she wanted to view the final property as soon as possible, as she had a packed schedule.

The last house, a renovated Georgian property, had a large garden, which overlooked the Thames. Petals of sunlight glinted across the water. The river always instilled a sense of calm in Grace. A tug chugged along contentedly, and a couple of rowers glided through the water as effortlessly as the swans which swam close to the shore. Close to her prospective home. The house was a good size. She liked the old stone fireplace and original cornicing in the high-ceilinged rooms. The kitchen was largely oak and contained an AGA cooker (Grace was looking forward to baking again, as she had done as a child, with her mum). The house was promising. She already started to plan which room she would convert into an office. Tamara offered to grant the client more time to spend viewing the property on her own, but Grace instructed the agent to remain with her (as opposed to spending time with her driver) in case she had any questions.

"Let me walk you to your car," Grace kindly remarked, as they came out of the house. "This property ticks a lot of boxes. I will be in touch by the end of the week, to let you know whether we can move forward or not. I'm terribly sorry that I'm unable to discuss things more with you now but I have another important meeting I need to attend to. Thank you so much for your time and help today."

Tamara was ushered towards her car. All she could do was smile and wave at Marshal. He waved and smiled back.

Ships that pass in the night. He thought. *Was the phrase from Longfellow?*

Tamara promised herself that she would text the driver, once his contract with her client had ended. What business was it of hers whether she arranged to see James or not anyway?

He's fit and fun.

"Ciao, for now," Tamara said. She wasn't quite sure if she was going to describe the model as "nice" or "a bit of a bitch" when she returned to the office.

Ciao, forever, Grace thought as she offered up her best fake smile and turned her back on the Audi TT and bottle blonde estate agent.

"Where to now?" Marshal asked, as Grace climbed into the back of his car again.

"Somewhere special I hope."

The sun came out even more.

Grace directed Marshal to turn off into a tree-lined road, towards the end of Chiswick High St, and park outside a parade of shops. They got out the car and walked towards an empty outlet, in between a bakery and bridal shop. A wonderfully camp letting agent, Andrew, stood outside. He was dressed in his best Dior suit. His smile showed off his recently capped teeth, and not a dyed hair on his head seemed out of place. The former fashion student did his best to contain his excitement on meeting the glamourous – fabulous – model. But his best wasn't good enough. Grace Wilde was a veritable starlet. Or had been. The letting agent didn't quite know what to compliment the model on first – her hair, flawless skin or kitten heels. It took an almost heroic amount of restraint, not to ask the model about the rumours concerning her and Zac Efron. He blushed on occasion and nearly even swooned at one point, when chatting to "the goddess," as he had described her to colleagues in the office. Grace was patient and obliging in dealing with her number one fan. She answered a few questions and struck a comical pose for a selfie. Andrew proved professional, however, after his moment, and knew his brief in relation to the property. They went inside and, after a preliminary discussion, Grace asked if she could view the site without the agent present.

"Do you mind if I just show my friend around first? I may well have some questions for you afterwards, should you be free for a coffee."

Any disappointment Andrew felt at being temporarily dismissed was tempered by the fact that he would soon be having coffee with Grace Wilde. He duly sent out a barrage of messages to his WhatsApp group and giddily replied to the responses as he waited outside the shop.

The space was almost the size of a tennis court. The pinewood flooring had recently been polished, and the smell of fresh paint filled the air. Grace took a breath, surveyed the scene and beamed. She was almost as excited as Andrew had been, when meeting the model.

"I'm opening a bookshop," Grace said, with visible pleasure and anticipation. "I know there's a temptation to think that it'll be a white elephant or money pit, but I think I can make it work. I've sweated over the business plan and an old friend, who has worked in both retail and the book trade, will manage things on a day to day level."

Grace proceeded to chat about how she had already started to book authors to speak at the shop. Her manager was liaising with schools and local businesses to generate account customers too.

"I'd love to get William Dalrymple here for our opening. He's a local, when he's not in India. If you haven't already read his books, you should… A third of the shop will be devoted to children's books… I should talk to you and Oliver about stocking our History section… I want to create a bay for staff picks and signed books… I've already started making a list for the Classics bay too… I'm even looking forward to the papercuts from the books… We're going to call the shop The Model Reader. My manager thinks we should get some good PR, both in the local papers and trade press… So, what do you think?"

It was Marshal's turn to be rapt. His mouth was open, agape. In some ways, she was living out his dream, in opening a bookshop. He couldn't help but be struck by Grace's infectious enthusiasm and enterprise. They shared a look. It wasn't ardour. It was something finer. It involved a shared sense of humour and respect.

"This all sounds wonderful, Grace. It's not often that I get to say that I envy or admire anyone. Dislike, yes. But envy, no," Marshal remarked, imagining how the space would look, teeming with books and customers.

"I'd love you to come to the launch in a month's time."

"I'd be honoured," Marshal replied, worried that he might have sounded a little sarcastic in his response. But for once, he wasn't being sarcastic. "I promise to be one of your first customers, when you open your doors. And I'll buy plenty of books."

"It's a date," Grace said, feeling a little shy and awkward as the words hung in the air, like a reverberating twang from a broken cello string. The throwaway line was suddenly infused with meaning. She realised that, should he have asked her on a date, she would have said yes. Marshal felt awkward too, remembering his promise to Porter. He had a history of breaking hearts, but he was averse to breaking his word.

13.

Grace took Andrew for a coffee to discuss various details relating to her lease. She invited the letting agent to the launch party for the shop. He accepted, nearly breaking his biscotti in excitement as he did so. He gleefully thought about who he might invite to attend the event with him – and who he might be able to upset by snubbing them.

After the meeting, Marshal drove Grace to another estate agency, to arrange more viewings. They then headed back west, towards Windsor. Grace continued to chat about the bookstore, often asking Marshal's opinion.

"I hope you don't mind me interrogating you. The truth is that I've barely told any of my friends and family about the venture. I also value your opinion."

"It's okay, I'm fine to talk shop," Marshal replied, although he was unsure as to whether Grace picked-up on his bad pun.

During the drive back, the pair chatted about some of the books and authors that *The Model Reader* should stock and champion.

Grace mentioned she had already ordered Bernard Malamud, Graham Greene, Flaubert, Nathaniel Hawthorne and special hardback editions of Jane Austen.

Marshal mentioned George Macdonald Fraser, Albert Camus, Steven Saylor, Harlan Coben and Barbara Tuchman. Should she be devoting a bay to philosophy then the shop should make sure it stocked key titles by David Hume, Nietzsche and Kierkegaard. When Grace quizzed him about history books to promote, he recommended Gary Sheffield's *Forgotten Victory*, Adam Zamoyski's *1812*, Ronald Syme's *The Roman Revolution* and Alex von Tunzelmann's *Red Heat*.

Grace also confided in Marshal as to why she was opening the shop, realising as she spoke that she hadn't told anyone before. The car became Marshal's confessional again. But this time he didn't mind.

"What little education I have, I owe to books. I'm paying something forward – or paying it back. Before I was signed-up as a model I was signed-up to go to university and study literature. I promised myself I would carry on studying, whilst modelling. But the trade can get its claws into you. Agents want your soul. You try to keep parts of your life sacred, like your family, friends and interests. But you have to give up your Horcruxes in the end," Grace argued, talking to herself as much as Marshal. He nodded in sympathy, pretending to know what a Horcrux was. "Others may argue that I have had a privileged life. That it's been a fairy tale or dream. But dreams can turn into nightmares. People who promise you heaven often deliver up hell."

Grace momentarily paused – and winced slightly – as she remembered going to the hotel suite with the film director Winston Royce. Royce was being hailed by the critics – and progressive liberal elite – as being the next Roman Polanski. His latest movie, telling the story of three women on the Oregon Trail, had won an award in Europe and been given a standing ovation at the Sundance Film Festival. Royce was lauded for championing young black actors, and his fans bullied and behaved like a lynch mob towards anyone who criticised the director for historical inaccuracies and his abusive tantrums on set. He was an artist. A genius. As much as Royce said he was from "the streets," they were the streets in and around Long Island. He could be charming, as well as abusive. The director met Grace at a party in Manhattan. He said that she should come up to his suite. That mutual friends would be joining them. Grace was keen to discuss the possibility of writing a screenplay (Royce was slightly taken back, as models would normally do anything to act in one of his films). He poured her a strong drink and went into the toilet. He re-appeared, wearing a robe, and suggested that their mutual friends must be tied-up. Grace could still smell his cologne – and sweat. She could still see the rock of cocaine stuck in his wiry nostrils and the white line around his face, where his fake tan ended. It was like he was wearing a mask. She could still feel his chubby, clammy hands on her shoulders, as Royce approached Grace and told her he would make her "a star". She shivered, in the backseat, as she felt his cold wedding ring on her skin. The entitled director screwed his face up in derision when the model rejected him. He grabbed her more firmly, his eyes glazed with lust. Carnality. The tension in the suite congealed even more, like a scab. Grace grew frightened. Royce asserted that no one said "no" to him. His tone grew firmer. Menacing. For a moment, she believed that he would assault her. But a moment was more than enough. A knock on the door, from room service, saved her. Grace sobbed, in relief and sorrow, as she rushed out and went home. After she vomited, Grace showered – but she was unable to wash away the memory. Rather it seemed like she was rubbing the nightmare into her. She sobbed again, observing the bruises on her shoulders, from where he had grabbed her. She asked herself if she had somehow led him on. If she should blame herself. If she was the perpetrator instead of the victim. Grace spoke to her agent about the incident. He advised her to remain quiet. Nothing actually happened, he argued. Royce would sue if she made any damaging allegations. A pack of lawyers would descend upon her like jackals. The industry would rally around the liberal poster boy. The supporter of Antifa was also friends with the Clintons. Her career would suffer. The agent declined to mention that his would too.

"My life could have been different," Grace remarked to Marshal, breaking out of her trance. "Instead of being propositioned by lecherous photographers, I could have attended university and been propositioned by lecherous academics," the model joked, but did not laugh.

Before Marshal could reply, Grace's phone rang. She apologised and said she needed to answer it. He didn't mean to pry, but he couldn't help but overhear half the conversation.

"I flew in yesterday. I'm sorry I haven't had time to speak to you properly… There was one property that felt homely. It's by the river… Thankfully I can afford it as I sold my apartment in Manhattan, and prices there are as inflated as London. The strong dollar has helped too… Yes, I'm still coming to the party tomorrow. Am looking forward to catching up with you... No, I'm not bringing anyone. Nor do I wish to leave with anyone, so there's no need to try and set me up with a Prince Charmless... I've booked a hotel in the area, so there's no need to put me up. My aunt arranged a driver for me... I can get to you early. Let's make some time for each other, before the evening starts in earnest... How are your parents?"

Grace finally hung up the phone. It was good to hear her friend's voice again. It was like medicine. There were few people in New York, who she was leaving behind, she could call a friend.

"That was Olivia. She's hosting the party in Witney, tomorrow. I've already sent you the address. I am planning on getting there a bit earlier now. I'm not sure how late I'll be staying yet, however."

Grace was looking forward to meeting her friend, but not necessarily looking forward to meeting her friend's friends. She could picture the scene now, of men, married or otherwise, trying to chat her up. Their egos wouldn't allow them to admit that Grace wasn't interested or attracted to them. Or if they did, they would consider her frigid or a bitch. The women at the party may well scowl at her more though, believing that Grace was attempting to steal their man and demand to be the centre of attention. But she would paint a smile on her face, after putting on her make-up, and survive.

But life should be more than just about surviving.

"Would you like to come to the party with me?" Grace asked, after taking a breath, as if she were about to plunge into the sea. Not only might he be able to ward off some unwanted advances, if people mistook Marshal for her boyfriend – but the truth was she wanted to spend more time with him. "I could use the company, and I wouldn't just want you to wait in the car all evening. Olivia says that high society will be attending, as well as various celebrities, but don't let that put you off. I've booked us a couple of rooms in a local hotel, so I can order us a cab at the end of the night. We can pick up the car in the morning. You will then be able to have a drink at the party. I'm not sure I will be able to suffer high society if sober, so I shouldn't expect you to do so too."

Marshal experienced flashbacks to similar parties he had attended as an officer. He could feel the stiff collar again rubbing against his neck, like a Redcoat wearing a stock. He could hear a thousand wine glasses clink together, sounding like crashing wave – about to capsize his boat. He pictured his head nodding like a marionette, his smile resembling a rictus, as he listened to modish or fascistic opinions. He flinched a little as he imagined hearing shrill laughter or plummy guffaws – or conversations about holidaying in Tuscany. Attending a party, by the good and the great, was the last thing that Marshal felt like doing now.

"I'd love to come, thanks."

Marshal realised he had said yes not because of anything he owed Porter, but because he wanted to do Grace a favour. He knew her enough to want to get to know her more. She also made him laugh. And he found himself laughing with rather than at her, which was a refreshing change.

14.

Marshal retreated into the guesthouse when they returned to the house. Sleep beckoned to him, like a succubus, but he drank a strong, black coffee and opened his laptop. The image of Grace kept inserting itself in his head, and her unaffected laughter echoed in his ears. But he did his best to banish visions of the model, like a monk endeavouring to banish tempting, intemperate thoughts.

He proceeded to enlarge his intelligence picture of the Albanians. He memorised key home and business addresses. He researched the locations of CCTV cameras in the areas. He once attended a lecture by a former MI5 operative, who briefed the room on building-up an intelligence picture. The more information he had, the better informed his decisions would be. He had to study his enemy's distribution network, funding, recruitment process, hierarchy, known associates and operational procedures.

Marshal closed the blinds, ensured that the door was locked and opened the aluminium case that contained the Glock. He clasped the hard, coal-black weapon, with its pimpled grip, wanting it to feel familiar in his hand again. Wanting it to feel part of him, an extension of his arm and soul. He rehearsed the process of removing the gun from its shoulder holster and fixing the suppressor several times. The action needed to become muscle memory, second nature. All thoughts of Grace disappeared, as he pictured Rugova and Baruti – framed within the sight of the Glock. Marshal couldn't hesitate when he confronted the Albanians, as they wouldn't hesitate to kill him. He was willing to pull the trigger. He had the heart, or lack of heart, to do so. The faces of the Taliban he cut down didn't haunt him at night, but rather they hung in his mind like trophies on a mantlepiece. Marshal remembered his grandfather always kept a loaded Webley pistol in a drawer by his bed. He argued that he wanted to protect himself, should he encounter any intruders. There was a significant part of the veteran soldier which desired to be burgled, in order to fire the weapon again.

"The bastards deserve to die."

A memory slotted itself into Marshal's thoughts, like a knife sliding in between two ribs. Helmand. A village. The air, even in the shade, felt like a furnace. A routine patrol turned into an ambush. Marshal and two of his men – Cooper and Jarrod – were taking fire in a market square, as they took cover behind a brace of stone benches. They were caught in the crossfire, between three Taliban fighters positioned behind a wall at the end of the market and a sniper (or snipers) firing down on them from a first-floor window. The dead body of Marshal's Corporal, Billy Tyson, lay at his feet. His freckled, shocked face was as white as a snowdrop. A round had ripped out his throat, nearly severing his head. The tough, bawdy Ulsterman had been deployed in Helmand at the same time as Marshal. The two men drank together, played darts together and fought together. Tyson had saved his Captain's life on more than one occasion. But Marshal had to devote himself to the living rather than to the dead.

Bullets zipped through the air and chipped away at the stone benches. Cooper had radioed for support but there was no way of knowing when it would arrive. The village was a viper's nest, full of enemy riflemen and IEDs.

Marshal calculated that they would eventually be sitting ducks. They would have died already, if the sniper was more proficient or one of the enemy possessed an RPG. He decided to go on the attack. The officer first handed his rifle to Jarrod, who had just exhausted his ammunition. He next asked his men to provide a burst of cover fire, before scrambling out from behind the benches. Bullets kicked-up dust around his feet as he raced towards the end of the square. As he reached cover, Marshal let out a blood-curdling scream and howled out, "Man down! Man down!" He wanted the sniper to believe he had injured him, that he was no longer a threat. Sweat drenched his grimy face and stung his eyes. His throat felt like it was lined with sandpaper. Marshal drew his pistol – a Glock

17 – and made his way through the narrow streets, avoiding any potential line of sight with the sniper, towards the building where the Taliban was positioned. Although his blood was up Marshal controlled his breathing. He stealthily entered the apartment building and slowly climbed the stairs, mindful that if he trod on a creaking step, he may well alert the enemy to his position. A burst of fire from the Taliban's weapon could easily go through the plaster wall parallel to the staircase and cut him down.

The good news was that there was only one sniper present. The bad news was he spotted the British soldier out the corner of his eye as Marshal stood in the doorway. He was quick to pull his rifle around and aim it at the infidel. But not quick enough. The first shot from Marshal's pistol ricocheted off the AK47, rendering it useless, and struck the sniper's bicep. The second shot tore a hole in his gut, flooring him. The wound was serious, but not necessarily fatal. Marshal approached the sniper. The Afghani could have been no older than twenty. His attempt at a beard was almost comical. Rage had been replaced by a piteous expression. A couple of tears streamed down his cheeks. He said a couple of words in his native language, before uttering, "Mercy, mercy." The young captive could well prove a source of valuable intel. Marshal shot the adolescent twice in the face and then, from his elevated position, threw a grenade at the remaining Taliban behind the wall.

The bastards deserved to die.

The two women were fussed over, and not purely because of their attractiveness. When Victoria and Grace arrived at the Italian restaurant, *Garibaldi's*, they were welcomed with open arms by the owner, Roberto, who had an uncanny resemblance to Eli Wallach. Porter had recently provided Roberto with help, which had saved the establishment from going under. The women were shown to a quiet table at the back. A complimentary carafe of Chianti and a plate of antipasto were waiting for them. Dean Martin played in the background. The walls were decorated with wood panelling and pictures of

Garibaldi, Augustus Caesar, Caprera – and Tony Bennett. Freshly cut flowers and wicker placemats furnished each table. The aesthetic of the restaurant wouldn't have looked out of place in the seventies, eighties or two thousand and thirty. Some of the remaining décor appeared kitsch, or just plain cheap, but the food and service were excellent.

Victoria invited her niece out for dinner because she imagined Grace might want to spend the night away from her driver. She hadn't been terribly impressed by his presence the previous evening. They could also talk more freely if it was just the two of them. Ironically, Grace could barely stop thinking about Marshal throughout dinner. And when not privately musing upon the ex-soldier she would subtly interrogate her aunt about Marshal (as nonchalantly as possible, of course).

"His mother died when he was young, Oliver told me… James is estranged from his father, Donald. His father was disappointed in his son becoming a private military contractor, effectively a mercenary, after leaving the army. James was conversely disappointed in his father for the way he abrogated his responsibilities towards his grandfather. Donald advised his son not to throw his life away looking after the recent stroke victim, that he should just leave him in a care home."

Grace leaned forward over the table, rapt by her aunt's every word. Unwittingly or not she was building up her own intelligence picture of Marshal. The more information she had, the better informed her decisions would be.

Before Victoria had the opportunity to say anything else Roberto re-appeared, carrying a second complimentary carafe of wine.

"You must let us pay. I can, of course, get my revenge by leaving a generous tip," Victoria said, protesting as best she could.

"Your husband has already paid us, tenfold. The local authority – parasites – were going to raise our rent and rates again. Not even the Cosa Nostra extort money from small businesses the way the government does. They had already promised our restaurant space to Pizza Express. We argued that we had been part of the community for twenty years. That we had paid, without complaint, the extra rent and rate rises over the past five years. Oliver heard about our problem and calmly said, "Leave it with me. I'll fix things." I didn't hold out much faith, I must confess, but within a fortnight the council contacted us and said we would now experience a rate freeze, instead of a rate rise. I still don't know how he did it. Your husband was a godsend. He is a good man. The best of men. It's only natural that the wife of mister Oliver should be the best of women. And the best of women must have the best wine," Roberto exclaimed, gesticulating with his free hand, and filling the two glasses on the table.

"Well, you might not think that Oliver was the best of men if you had to sample his cooking. But thank you, Roberto."

The rosy-cheeked owner departed, thinking about which kind of special dessert he could ask his chef to cook-up for the two ladies.

"So, when did you first realise that uncle Oliver was a good man, or the best of men? You've never told me about when you first met. All I hear from my friends are tales of infidelity and divorce. It'll be nice to hear a story with a happy ending for once. Was it love at first sight?" Grace asked, enjoying the wine and briefly thinking about what she might wear for the party tomorrow night.

What would he like?

"Oh, I think it might have been loathing at first sight. He looked good in uniform, but most men look good in uniform. As well as swearing an oath to Queen and country, Guards officers also seemingly have a duty to be full of themselves when they receive their commissions. Some remain faithful to that duty until the day they die too. I only started to find Oliver interesting when he stopped trying to impress me. Being terrified of my father helped him behave himself... The main reason why I liked him, which he never realised, which only made me like him more, was that he made me laugh. He still does... But getting married doesn't mean it's happy ever after. If they gave out long-service medals for staying married in the army, they wouldn't have to cast too many... When he retired there was still a part of Oliver which remained remote. He became devoted to his work. It was like he had a mistress down in London. He argued that he was working hard to provide for me and the children, but I doubt if he even believed that himself. I'm still not quite sure what he did, during his time as a consultant. He said he provided financial services and advice on security. He certainly arranged drivers and close personal protection for clients," Victoria explained, thinking that part of her didn't want to know what her husband did. Semi-ignorance is bliss.

"Was there a moment when you knew Oliver was the one?" Grace asked, hoping the answer might prove as easy and obvious as two plus two equalling four. She felt moved and undeniably attracted to Marshal, earlier. It was when he had spontaneously recited Pushkin. If it had been a performance, then what a performance. He was like no one she had ever known. But if the melancholy in his features and voice were real – then he was like no one she had ever known. *I live on, alone and jaded.* Grace also recalled the appreciative (enamoured?) glint in his eye when she announced that she was opening the bookshop. He was genuinely happy for her. Had they shared their own moment?

"There may well be two answers to that question. The first was when Oliver said, in all earnestness, that if I gave the word, he would be willing to sacrifice his career in the army for me. I still remember the second moment vividly. We were having dinner with my family, and my father had also invited several senior officers over to meet Oliver. Halfway through the evening Oliver excused himself and went upstairs to use the bathroom. After being gone for some time I found him. My grandmother, who was staying with us at the time, had called out from having a nightmare and Oliver had popped into her room to make sure she was okay. I can still see him now, perched on the end of her bed, reading a Georgette Heyer novel to her. "He's a nice man, a keeper," she said to me the following morning. And one should always listen to one's grandmother, as well as one's aunt."

The garden was swathed in lambent moonlight. The stars shimmered like silver dollar fish on the surface of a black sea. The light shone in the darkness. The two men sat, satiated, on cushioned chairs. A small table sat between them, holding two tumblers filled with eighteen-year-old *Macallan* and a pair of ashtrays, containing *King of Denmark* cigars. The meal had been simple, but delicious. Porter had picked up a couple of fillet steaks from his local butchers and cooked them with some new potatoes and button mushrooms. For dessert, Victoria had whipped up some Eton Mess beforehand. It was one of her husband's favourites, as it reminded him of his childhood. Although they had just eaten their supper in the kitchen Porter was still dressed for dinner. The crease running down his trousers was straighter than a Roman road. Marshal fancied that someone could prick their finger and draw blood on the tip of his handkerchief, such was the sharpness on the point, which hung out of his breast pocket. He also noticed Porter's gleaming silver novelty cufflinks, of two shotgun cartridges – a present from his wife. Marshal was dressed more casually, in jeans, a blue polo shirt and white Reeboks (an unofficial uniform, of sorts, for some South-East Londoners).

The two former officers discussed ex-colleagues. Some had left the army, but more so they gossiped about those who had recently left their wives for younger women. Divorce had cost some of them their dignity, or more damagingly half their pensions and their homes. Porter also mentioned a fellow ex-Guards officer who had been awarded a peerage. He had first contacted the Tory party to secure his entry into the Lords, but they had been lukewarm in their response. So, the former General approached the Liberal Democrats (albeit there was little that was liberal or democratic about the party). "He has no shame, but he does have a peerage," Porter tartly remarked. "I understand he's regimental about signing-in each day at the at the Palace of Westminster, whilst keeping the cab running and turning back round to go to lunch – which he duly puts on expenses."

"Have you never thought about going into politics?" Marshal asked, refilling their glasses with the Sancerre his host had liberated from the special corner of his wine cellar. Violet sat by his chair, either from devotion or she thought the guest might drop some food on the floor.

"By God, no," Porter exclaimed, nearly choking on a piece of steak. "Perhaps if I was more dishonest, if I held fewer, or no, principles, I might be able to consider it. If I only possessed a will to embezzle – or could be bought by a lobbyist. I am not sure I have the energy to feign concern about climate change – or hold passionate opinions about subjects I know or care nothing about. I can't bring myself to say a woman is a man, just because that's the way she feels. If only I was as intelligent as David Lammy, as un-shrill Anna Soubry, as honourable as Grant Shapps, as honest as John McDonnell, as competent as Chris Grayling and as wise as Diane Abbott then I might be tempted to go into politics. But I'm content to remain retired. Yet you still have a fair amount of your working life ahead of you, James. Have you thought about coming out of retirement?"

"I'm good for nothing. Which is why I'll probably continue to do nothing," Marshal replied, shrugging his shoulders. The soul of insouciance. "I flirted with the idea of being a journalist at one point, believe it or not. But journalists tend to compose more tweets than articles these days. I would have ended up preaching to the converted, or throwing pearls before swine, I imagine. Or am I supposed to get a desk job somewhere, with a bank or at the MOD? In the Paras, I was serving beside men next to me who would watch your back, who would sacrifice their lives for me. If I worked for the civil service the men next to me would watch Celebrity Big Brother, and begrudgingly sacrifice the use of their phone charger. I say this with a sense of remorse rather than pride, but the British Army is one of the last bastions of a sense of honour and professionalism in the country. After signing up to the Paras, signing up to anything else would prove an anti-climax."

Talk about Marshal's future, in relation to the Albanians, was conspicuous by its absence over dinner. Porter judged that his guest would speak about the issue when he wanted to. If he brought up the subject, or provided some advice, the fixer might unwittingly convey acceptance or encouragement of a violent course of action. But Porter sensed that the soldier's course of action was already set in stone. "If I don't do something about it, who will?" he had argued, during their meeting at the National Liberal Club. Although Marshal was largely free from vanity, he would not be able to escape his pride.

Porter got up from his chair and turned up the electric lamp, which hung over the two men on the porch.

"It's getting colder. We can't just rely on the whisky to keep us warm. But tell me, how was the temperature in the car today? Did you have to turn the heating on? I hope Grace wasn't too cold towards you. Please don't judge her too harshly if she was. Victoria told me that she has had a rough year. Quite rightly, she doesn't like or trust most men. I don't either. I think coming back home will be good for her, however. If it's any consolation, Grace mentioned she enjoyed your company earlier."

"The London air must have made her light-headed," Marshal drily replied, although he smiled on the inside.

"You will be pleased to know too that you'll be freed from your obligation early. Grace said that, once you return from Oxfordshire the day after tomorrow, she will arrange her own car."

Marshal tried to act pleasantly surprised, but his performance wasn't wholly convincing. The only thing he was surprised at was his prospective sadness at not seeing Grace again. If he had been told the same news the previous night, he would have felt satisfied. Free. But he now thought about suggesting to Porter that he would be fine with driving his niece for longer. He thought about wording something similar to Grace, tomorrow morning. But he was split, like a broken host. In a time of war, you can have either guns or butter. You can't have both. Marshal couldn't be in two places at once. He couldn't devote himself to Grace and the Albanians, as much as it sometimes felt like he led a dual existence.

I need to go back to London. To go back for good.

Porter got up again, this time to pop into the kitchen and fetch more ice. Marshal felt his phone vibrate in his pocket. A part of him wanted it to be a text from Grace. He just wanted to know she was okay.

Hi. It was fun meeting you today. You said you were used to fast women, so I thought I'd drop you a quick message. Lol. Tamara. Xx

Marshal didn't reply, but nor did he delete the message either.

15.

It was now after midday. The weather was unseasonably warm. Sweltering. The sun stung. Marshal glugged down a bottle of mineral water and waited by the car, for Grace.

Although Victoria had invited Marshal over for breakfast, he politely declined. Instead, he had half a packet of cigarettes and an apple. He also wanted to prove to himself that he had the restraint not to see Grace. To deny himself.

Marshal continued to work. He began to consider how he could hurt the organisation he was up against. The NCA couldn't extract any intelligence through enhanced interrogation techniques. But he could. Martin Elmwood would be unable to give the Albanians a taste of their own medicine – and torch their businesses. But he could. Marshal stared intently at the laptop, with a picture of Luka Rugova and Viktor Baruti on it. Boring or burning a hole in it.

He also perused the news headlines, in between bouts of research. A fifteen-year-old black youth had been stabbed in Newham. The slaying of Samuel Diop was gang-related, it was reported. Samuel had been murdered on his way home from dropping off a delivery of cocaine to an IT consultant in Shoreditch. Samuel's parents said that he was a sweet boy, "who wouldn't hurt a fly" (despite having assaulted a pregnant female teacher when he was fourteen). He dreamed of playing football for his favourite team, Arsenal. He loved rap music. His hero was someone called 50 Cent. Even if the Albanians were innocent of any involvement in the killing, Marshal was happy to punish them for the crime.

Beads of sweat formed on his temple. Violet panted at his feet. He idly recalled the opening line of *On Her Majesty's Secret Service*:

"It was one of those Septembers when it seemed that the summer would never end."

During the previous night, Porter had asked him about the extent of his ambition, what he wanted from life. Marshal remembered a scene from the spy novel. Bond was in a meeting with an expert on genealogy and family mottos. The expert mentioned that Bond's family motto was, "The World is not Enough." For Marshal, however, the world was too much. He didn't want much from life, and he didn't have much to give either.

Grace appeared. He drank in the sight of her. She was wearing a light cotton floral print dress with very expensive, very sexy ankle-high black boots. For a moment he stood entranced, dumbstruck. Even her knees and elbows were pretty. Prettier even than Anne Hathaway's, he speculated. Marshal remembered his promise to Porter, partly because he regretted making it.

"Hi, how are you?" Grace said, visibly pleased to see him. There was a vibrancy, electricity, in her being, as though today was the first day of the rest of her life.

Better for seeing you, Marshal thought.

Grace had thought of the ruse the night before. In order to sit in the front with Marshal, she asked if she could charge up her tablet in the passenger seat. She wanted to develop a more personal, as opposed to professional, relationship with her driver.

Marshal did his utmost, which wasn't quite good enough, not to stare across at Grace's chest – at the cross which hung down from her necklace. Was she Catholic? If he knew the answer to that there were dozens of other questions he need not ever ask. He thought it might seem odd if he just came out and asked her, for seemingly no reason. He tried to think of another, subtler, question that might provide him with the answer but suitably concentrated on his driving when he nearly missed his turn off at the right junction.

Grace quickly cleared her inbox and then started to chat to Marshal about the party, and its host. Olivia was married to a hedge fund manager, Simon Yale.

"Although he frequently tells people he's more than a hedge fund manager. Simon has told me what he does more than once, although I can never remember any details. I'm not sure if it's because I'm confused or bored... He calls himself a "Master of the Universe, like Sherman McCoy" – although he's never actually read Bonfire of the Vanities. His superpower is his arrogance, although he may be deemed modest in relation to some of the guests at the event tonight... Simon says he's invited George Osborne, Jemima Khan and Damien Hurst... I hope you don't mind, but when we get to the house, I'm going to abandon you for a while, as I'd like to catch up with Olivia."

"That's fine. I would say you could introduce me to the Witney set, but I fear I would then have to abandon them," Marshal replied, before yawning. "God, I'm yawning even just thinking about Jemima Khan and Damien Hurst opening their mouths."

Grace laughed. Marshal thought how she had a lovely laugh and smile. Even if she used them more, they would still be precious. Her gaze lingered on him (she thought he didn't notice, but he did). He was a puzzle she couldn't quite work out. But wanted to work out.

Marshal switched on his country music playlist. They passed by lush green fields, under a scintillating sky, listening to Hank Williams, The Dixie Chicks, Garth Brooks and Dolly Parton.

"But I ain't been home in I don't know when
If I had it all to do over again
Tonight I'd sleep in my old feather bed.
What I wouldn't give for a little bitty taste
Of mama's homemade chocolate cake
Tennessee homesick blues running through my head."

He covertly glanced at her smooth, tanned legs in the sunshine – and the way she tapped her booted foot to several songs. She would remark, within a few bars of a track starting, "good song" or "great song" – and then mouth some of the lyrics.

She was even familiar with Shawn Colvin.

I think I'm in love, he joked to himself.

Marshal wondered what he would say if she asked him if he was a Catholic. Was he lapsed? Non-practising? Devout? Deficient? He had collected a couple of sacraments, like minor service medals, which nearly everyone received. Ironically, he believed that life was sacred. He was anti-capital punishment and, though he was pilloried for it and treated like a heretic, anti-abortion. But doubt always bit into him, like a serpent that wouldn't let go. Like barbed wire coiled around his colon.

Marshal remembered the chapel at their base in Helmand and it's make-shift altar. The smell of incense took him back to his childhood, when his mother was alive. The pearlescent candles crowned with tranquil flames. A pine crucifix stood by the entrance. Sometimes the figure of Christ, with his head tilted to the side, looked like he was indifferent to the world. Shrugging his shoulders. At other times he appeared tortured. Pitiful and pitying. The chapel door was always open. But Marshal always walked by rather than walked in. If he killed a Talib on Saturday was he supposed to confess his sin on Sunday? If he hadn't done anything wrong, if he had saved others while damning the enemy, why should he prostrate himself before a non-existent, or ambivalent, God?

When Marshal walked by the chapel, he often saw a fellow officer from his regiment, Cameron Bell, inside, praying. Bell had a face as shiny as a new penny. He was quiet, thoughtful. Non-confrontational. Marshal often wondered why Bell had elected to become a soldier, until he heard that he came from a military family, one far more established and distinguished than his own. Most of the squaddies thought the officer was queer and, when it was discovered that he composed war poetry, they nicknamed him "Wilfred", after the WWI poet. The Paras was perhaps not the best place to trumpet that you were a Catholic, given the experiences of the Troubles, but Bell never shied away from his faith. It shaped his daily life. Marshal was surprised that religion didn't play a larger part in the lives of his fellow soldiers. Death stalked them, like a shadow, every time they left the base. He considered that more might have hedged their bets. Or perhaps they kept their faith hidden, like money in a sock drawer. Maybe they didn't want to show weakness, albeit Marshal judged that Bell's faith was a source of strength and consolation. Some men would call out to God, or their mothers, when wounded or dying. Marshal briefly mused upon who he would call out to in the end.

He had got drunk with Bell one evening. They spoke about the lack of helicopters, the Battle of Arnhem and T. S. Eliot's *The Wasteland*. After God knows how many drinks, the studious officer spoke about his faith, with some subtle or not prompting from Marshal.

"I go to the chapel to speak to God. It's quiet there, so I can hear him. I know the men may scoff behind my back, but when I speak to God, I feel like I'm speaking to the best part of myself... Guilt is good. It teaches us not to make the same mistake, or commit the same sin, twice. Guilt is God. Proof of conscience. And a conscience is proof of the divine... I feel better for the act of confession and contrition. My heart – and body even – feels unburdened afterwards. You are a Catholic too. You must understand, no?" Bell, a former Ampleforth pupil, asked, laying a hand on Marshal's arm. He replied that he half understood.

Half the time when he passed by the chapel and observed Bell in prayer Marshal felt a wave of envy. He wished that faith, rather than drink, could nourish and sustain him. He wished that prayer could act an anti-biotic to his despair. But how many Hail Marys would he have to utter before he could atone for his crimes and wipe the slate clean? He would have to spend a year praying, to start chipping away at just one of his mortal sins? But would it not be worth it in the end?

At other times, his skin prickled with scorn for Bell. Was he not experiencing a state of smugness rather than serenity? Was he not merely telling himself that God was forgiving him? It wasn't devotion he was witnessing, but delusion. In Sunday School, Marshal was told that God loved Man because he was His creation. But if Man created God, do we not love Him for the same reason?

"A penny for your thoughts," Grace said, hoping to snap Marshal out of his trance, as she prompted him to crawl forward, whilst stuck in traffic.

"You may well be overestimating their value. I was just thinking that I may need to find another route, if I can't get through this."

"It's up to you. I trust you."

Grace rightly sensed that he was deflecting, but she appreciated why he might not want to discuss certain things. *"Without deceiving himself a man cannot live,"* she thought, recalling a quote from Turgenev.

Viktor Baruti sat in *The High Life*. He stirred his coffee four times and tapped his spoon on the side of his cup twice. As much as the Albanian appeared to be at peace, he had an itch he wanted to scratch. He could feel a pea beneath his mattress, preventing him from sleeping. The mysterious Englishman was still a conundrum. The intelligence officer had reached out to Junior "Windy" Gayle, an informant in Onslow's gang. Gayle was a low-level dealer in the West Indian's organisation, who Baruti paid in cocaine. The Albanian had contacted his informant to find out if he knew whether Onslow had recently recruited some outside help. A white Englishman, probably an ex-soldier. As far as Gayle knew his boss hadn't employed anyone new, but his life wouldn't be living if it turned out that he had misinformed the Albanian. And so, Gayle hedged his bets and said he had heard a rumour that Onslow was in the process of recruiting more men, but couldn't be certain. Baruti asked his informant who would know, for certain, whether a specialist had been recruited. Gayle gave him a name of one of Onslow's lieutenants, Curtly Lambert. The kryetar debated whether to abduct Lambert and extract the truth. He needed to know. The more information he had, the better informed his decisions could be. Should the Englishman be working for his rivals, Baruti wondered whether he could be bought? Most people could be bought, but not everyone. Baruti believed he could not be bought himself – or forced to turn on his friend and employer. His krye was his brother. They had been through much together, helped build an empire together. Whether the Englishman was working for another outfit or not, Baruti would still try and play the alchemist. Turn lead into gold, a problem into an asset. The Albanian would find the stranger and run a background check on him, to assess if he could be recruited. An English enforcer could prove valuable to the organisation. He could pay off his blood debt with someone else's blood. If he was a kindred spirit, and possessed a predilection for violence, the Englishman might even enjoy his new job, Baruti surmised. Bishka and Baruti would not be happy about their attacker avoiding punishment, but he wasn't put on the planet to make those underlings happy. But first things first. They needed to track him down, before anything else could happen. The kryetar had sent out a priority message that his men should remain vigilant and observant. He also checked the app on his phone to ensure that Bisha and Bashkim were patrolling the right neighbourhood.

The sound of a long-limbed escort, wearing a corset dress and stripper heels, walking across the dancefloor made him glance up from his phone. She sniffed, fixed her dress into place and wiped her mouth, having just come out of Rugova's office. Baruti wondered how much force it would take to kill a woman, through tightening a corset. He pictured her eyes bulging, her scarlet lips turning blue.

Rugova had been celebrating their recent success. Baruti had been in a meeting with his friend earlier in the day. Their business model was still going strong. By buying in bulk directly from the Columbians, and avoiding middlemen where possible, they kept their product at a cheaper price, by passing on savings to their customers. The margins were still attractive. The nightclub, and other satellite enterprises, were also performing well.

"At this rate, we'll be able to afford to go legit soon," Rugova said, chuckling at his own joke and hoovering up a line of merchandise.

They finally arrived at the gated property. The drive was long and straight, flanked by trees. The scene reminded Marshal of pictures of old slave plantation estates in Virginia. The house at the end of the road was decidedly modern, however. The building was wrapped in tinted glass, supported by ribs of steel, roofed with solar panels and partly set on stilts. The building was coated with a special self-cleaning lacquer, whatever that was – and shone in the pristine sunlight as though the cellophane had just been removed from the dream home. The main house was surrounded by a glass-walled squash court, a tennis court and kidney-shaped swimming pool. The heavily chlorinated water smelled and looked like bleach. Simon never grew tired of telling people how much the house cost, and that his architect had also designed houses for Tony Blair and Angelina Jolie. The house had been shortlisted for various awards – and had won a special "Green Medal" for its investment in sustainability. A couple of old university friends had sat on the panel which announced the prize. Grace thought that the house resembled those she had seen in Hollywood and Malibu, owned by movie moguls and film stars with more money than sense. Marshal thought the house could have belonged to a Bond villain. Or Bono. A large, unsightly bronze sculpture, that looked like a stick of rhubarb which had seen better days, stood outside the main entrance to the house. The installation, designed by the third most renowned gender fluid artist in the country, was called "Progress".

It seemed that several party guests had already arrived. Marshal mused how his Jaguar was the runt of the litter in the designated car parking area, given the number of Bentleys, Aston Martins and Porches he was surrounded by. He could have been parked at a Premier League club training ground.

"I hope you don't mind, but people may mistake you for being my boyfriend this evening," Grace said, as she got out of the vehicle.

"There are worse fates."

"I just wouldn't want to make Violet jealous."

Marshal's half-smile turned into a full, piratical grin – as they shared another moment. A stream of people moved around them, like foaming water bending around a rock in a river.

16.

Evening.

The party had started. The house was lit up like a lava lamp from the nineteen seventies.

During the afternoon, Olivia welcomed Grace and, along with a bottle of Prosecco, took her for a walk in the woods. Olivia chatted to her old friend about the state of her marriage. Grace was already aware of some of Simon Yale's previous infidelities. Olivia had found incriminating evidence of another affair in the past month. She had confronted her husband and he explained that the affair had been meaningless, a one-night stand. He said he had got drunk and coked-up in London, after hearing about the death of his uncle. He had slept with someone who had come onto him. Seduced him. It meant nothing. "We shouldn't throw away what we have over a drunken mistake." Simon promised not to see her again – and he kept his word. Partly because he had a second mistress, which his wife was unaware of. Olivia said that she thought they were now through their "bad batch" and her husband was more attentive (he had recently bought her a new car and they were planning a trip to Tuscany). Simon was stressed from work and long hours meant he had to sometimes stay overnight in their flat in London. "We're going to be fine. We're happier than other couples I know." Grace nodded her head and offered her friend a shoulder to cry on as they sat on a stump in the woods. But she thought the lady was protesting too much. It wasn't only men who lied to themselves. Without deceiving herself a woman cannot live. The advice she wanted to offer was to keep any hard evidence of her husband's unfaithfulness, so Olivia could one day pass it onto a lawyer during divorce proceedings.

"But how about you? Have you got your eye on anyone? Or it's probably the case that someone has got their eye on you," Olivia posed to her friend. She had always been jealous of the attention her model friend attracted. She had hoped that Grace would be jealous of her, when she married Simon. But, annoyingly, she didn't feel any envy towards her.

"I'm keeping my eye out for Cupid, mainly to avoid his arrows rather than to step in front of one," Grace replied. She didn't mention her driver. There was nothing to say. Or was there?

Whilst Grace spent time with Olivia, Marshal waited in the car. He read and napped, which was a welcome return to his normal routine. His body felt stiff and sluggish when he woke. Part of him wanted to go for a run, feel his thighs burn and gulp down the country air. As much as he was looking forward to spending the evening with Grace, he was looking forward to returning to London too. He wanted a drink, whether a pint in his local pub or a large whisky back at his flat. He wanted a coffee back in *Hej*. Somehow other coffee tasted second-best. Grace was now waking him up and perking him up, instead of caffeine. He also wanted to book in time at a gun range.

Marshal swapped a few texts with Grace to arrange to meet her at the front of the house. He changed in the car. Apparently, the dress code was quite relaxed. He wore jeans, a shirt and suit jacket. For some reason, he felt nervous. His palms perspired. His heart rate was up. His insides fizzed, but he put that down to hunger. He never got nervous when going on dates, so why should he somehow be nervous now?

They met by the sculpture, but Marshal only had eyes for the natural beauty of Grace. She was wearing a dark blue *Roland Mouret* crepe fitted dress and *Kurt Geiger* heels. The cross around her neck glinted in the light, like a distant star. The lines of her figure cut through the air like the prow of a narrow ship gliding across the sea. Her bare skin – her shoulders, arms and shins – shimmered like Persian silk. Grace beamed, happy to see him. Her lips seemed fuller, and not just because of the lipstick. Her eyes were the window to a kind, humorous soul. Should Marshal have gone for a run, he might now have been weak at the knees. Desire – and something else – acted like bellows to stoke his being. He wasn't dead inside, for her.

"You look like Natasha Rostova, before a ball," he warmly remarked, after catching his breath.

The butterflies in her stomach fluttered some more, and she hoped she wasn't blushing too much. The model had received a torrent of compliments over the years. Too many to mention or remember. But she would remember that one. Grace wondered whether Marshal was more akin to Pierre or Prince Andrei from *War & Peace*. Perhaps he was like both. Perhaps he was like neither.

"And you're dressed like a hedge fund manager. You'll fit right in."

"There are worse fates. Although I can't quite think of any at the moment."

They walked through into the large ground floor area which hosted the party. Marshal's eyes darted around the room, examining possible threats, weapons and exits. Unfortunately, he also noticed salmon-pink leather sofas, chrome coffee tables, more gender fluid sculptures and the odd daubing by a painter who Simon proclaimed was "the new Basquiat". He stood on a peacock-blue tiled floor. The space resembled Ikea's latest showroom. Like the outside, the inside projected wealth rather than taste. Light sparkled off sequined dresses and jewellery, as if several disco balls hung from the ceiling. A pianist played in the corner, although she could barely be heard above the chattering classes.

The party spilled out onto the lawn and through the rest of the house, like poison ivy. Attractive catering staff, wearing faux satin French maid outfits, brought around glasses of Cristal champagne. Apparently, the caterers were the ones used by Harry and Megan at their wedding. Thin-lipped lawyers, balding financiers, smartphone-wielding lobbyists and media people (a classification which covered a multitude of sins) populated the room. Marshal wryly smiled, as he was indeed dressed like others at the party. He could have been mistaken for a Master of the Universe too, albeit he shuddered at the thought. He mused upon what the collective noun for lawyers might be. A pocket? And what about the collective name for media high-flyers? A slough? He read somewhere that the collective noun for feminists was a conceit. But surely that couldn't be right. Could it?

Non-white faces were conspicuous by their absence. The companies that guests ran had recently instigated small diversity schemes, however, which they were keen to publicise.

Alluring, statuesque women adorned their men, like accessories. They wore diaphanous, flowing gowns or chic cocktail dresses which seldom reached four inches above the knee. Outfits clung to gym-toned figures, like vacuum packed meat. Glossy, coiffured hair crowned bronzed, botoxed faces with taut, strained smiles. The women were achingly gorgeous, fantastically vain and wonderfully dull. There were, of course, exceptions which didn't disprove the rule. There was so much obtuse beauty in the room that it was somehow ugly. Overbearing. Marshal's eyes began to water from the fog of perfume which wafted over him.

The noise wasn't deafening enough, as he could still hear their cricket-like voices. He felt like his ears might burst, as if he were on a plane suffering from a change in cabin pressure. Throughout the evening Marshal would overhear more than one guest brag about how much their house cost, and how little they paid their staff. Various other gobbets of conversation made him wince or sigh.

"Anyone who voted for Brexit should be gassed, or at the very least they shouldn't be allowed to vote... Single-use plastics. They're evil. Wicked. Worse than knives or guns... I can't think of a greater crime than to have zero women directors on the shortlist for the Oscar. Can you think of something more unfair and egregious? I despair... You have to admire Mark Zuckerberg... There are dead people who probably pay more in tax than I do, thanks to my financial adviser. I would rather divorce my wife than fall out with him... Fucking Grenfell! I had to find a new cleaner and dog sitter when they rehoused the residents. What a disaster it was, trying to re-staff... I voted for the Green Party at the last election. Caroline Lucas knows what she's talking about."

Marshal could also intermittently hear the chopping sound of credit cards cutting up cocaine on mirrored table tops.

The consolation of being with Grace was soon taken away from him as Olivia approached and led her friend off, in order to introduce her to a top literary agent.

"You don't mind, do you, if I steal Grace away?" Olivia asked, without waiting for an answer. She considered him "just staff". Marshal couldn't quite decide whether his hostess had a sweet or sour face.

Grace mouthed "sorry" to him as she was dragged across the room, weaving her way through the glittering crowd. Olivia plonked her friend in front of the lauded agent, Julius Lavender. The Philip Green look-alike all but licked his lips, for various reasons, at the prospect of working with the stunning model. Lavender had slept with more than one aspiring novelist over the years, as writers grew starstruck with the famous agent, who could often be heard on Radio 4 or holding court at the Groucho Club. He was a "literary Svengali" and had "the Midas touch", according to his Wikipedia page, which he had his assistant setup. Lavender changed the subject when Grace asked about the possibility of arranging book signings with his clients (partly because he wouldn't be able to make any money out of the paltry events).

"Have you ever considered writing a book yourself? If you give me your number, we could discuss one or two projects over dinner next week."

"I am afraid I'm too busy at the moment to write a book."

"We could still go ahead. Don't be spooked, but I could always arrange a ghost-writer for you," the agent said, laughing at his own weak joke whilst placing a hand on her bare forearm.

Grace neither laughed nor smiled. Her skin crawled and she subtly recoiled from the sebaceous agent. She wanted to find Marshal, spend the night with him.

Marshal yawned and nursed a bottle of beer. Usually, he would have drunk heavily to take the edge of his mood at similar gatherings. But he was on duty. He might still need to drive Grace to her hotel. He searched around for a sight of her, not just out of a sense of duty. He was like a parent looking around for a line of sight on a child, or a child searching for a parent.

Unfortunately, instead of seeing Grace, Marshal caught sight of someone who looked remarkably like Lily Allen, stamping her foot and shouting at one of the serving girls. She was dressed in an even more ill-styled dress than the ill-informed singer, if that was at all possible.

"I said I wanted two olives in my fucking drink. Do you understand English? I could send out a tweet about your catering company and fucking destroy you."

The social media "influencer" was high on coke, and her own self-importance. She had been in meetings all day with her publicist, trying to decide whether to promote MAC or Bobbi Brown lipstick. She would duly recommend the company which paid the most.

The pianist finished her set – and a melange of modern pop music poured, like swill, out of the sound system. Marshal began to develop a headache. Perhaps he should get drunk. Vodka was like a magic potion, which gave him special powers to endure society. He felt like he had a thorn lodged in his frontal lobe. He desperately needed some fresh air – and a cigarette.

After smoking a couple of cigarettes outside, Marshal headed to his car to retrieve his portable phone charger. He came back to the house via a side entrance. From a distance, he noticed a few other guests by the side door, having a drink and smoking. He also saw one of the serving girls, attempting to collect glasses, and heard voices. Nicola could have been no older than twenty-one. She worked for the caterers to help pay for her studies. The comely girl was used to clients hitting on her, but they usually took things in good grace when she politely declined their advances, or subtly mentioned she had a boyfriend.

"Stay and party with us, out here. We've got champagne and coke. The only thing missing from the party is you," one of the men, Aaron Smyth, remarked. Smyth was around thirty years old and dressed in the obligatory jeans, shirt and suit jacket. He reminded Marshal of various chinless wonders in the civil service – and Ruperts he had encountered in the army. Smyth was sat around a table, with two friends. The first, Gareth Hunte, had the build of a fly-half. The second, Brad Masters, was tall and olive-skinned. He was strikingly handsome and physically imposing. He probably swam or rowed. Marshal thought he looked like an Argentinian polo player. He could have been a model for Marks & Spencer's Blue Harbour range of clothing.

Marshal quickly surveyed the scene. A few unused chairs were spread around the area. A couple of empty bottles of Cristal sat on the table, along with a couple of empty wine coolers, a credit card and the remnants of a line of cocaine. Hunte and Masters flanked Smyth. They seemed half cut and half high. Another figure stood apart from the trio, smoking, telling himself that the waitress could handle herself. That it was all just innocent fun. Smyth placed his hand on the serving girl's thigh as she leaned over to collect the empty bottles. She squirmed and wriggled free from his paw.

Smyth sized the newcomer up, with a thinly veiled look of contempt. The currency trader didn't recognise Marshal as being part of his circle. Although dressed smartly, his clothes were low-rent compared to others.

"Evening," Marshal said, turning towards the waitress. "Would you like some help taking those bottles inside?"

"Who are you? She's staying here, aren't you Nicola?" Smyth said, his voice dripping with arrogance and entitlement. When he screwed up his face the former Bullingdon Club member appeared pugnacious. He was used to getting his own way. He was used to women falling for his charms. The trader had rowed with his girlfriend earlier and left her back in their apartment in Chelsea. He would exact his revenge by sleeping with the young waitress, or someone else, tonight.

"You can fuck off inside though," Masters exclaimed, in a honking, New York accent, before sniffing up any detritus of cocaine stuck in his nostril.

"Nicola, would you like to go back inside?" Marshal asked, ignoring the would-be alpha male and his cohorts.

The girl nodded, visibly distressed.

"Get lost or get hurt," Hunte said, brusquely. The cocaine had kicked in. He was keen to either fight, or fuck someone, this evening, so as not to waste the high.

"You can't be one of Simon's friends in finance. If you were, you would be able to count better. There's three of us and one of you," Smyth asserted, running his hand through his long blond hair. His "mane", as he called it.

"I don't mind you fetching a couple more of your friends, if you want to make the odds more even," Marshal replied, with the flicker of a smile. His expression soon returned to one of even less thinly veiled contempt.

"You're funny," the trustafarian said, humourlessly. His features tightened, as the tension in the air congealed even more. The Master of the Universe was not used to being challenged or defied. Or, worse, treated as a joke.

"You're providing me with plenty of good material," Marshal replied, amiably and goadingly. He was fully prepared to engage with the trio, who were harassing the waitress.

His chair scraped across the floor as a riled Aaron Smyth quickly rose to his feet and approached the stranger. Hunte and Masters stood up in solidarity. The former Para didn't flinch as the currency trader closed in. Smyth believed he was a hawk to Marshal's dove. He wanted to affirm his superiority. But Smyth was boxing himself into a corner. He knew he couldn't now back down and lose face in front of his tribe.

The calm, confident half-smile on Marshal's face became more mocking than wistful. He was keeping his cool, in inverse relation to Smyth losing his. Yet, the ex-soldier's body remained a coiled spring. Ready to strike. He was a firework, ready to explode. All it needed was for someone to light the touch paper. The knight-errant was keen to protect the lady's honour. But, perhaps even more so, he was keen to beat the men in front of him to a pulp because he would enjoy it. Marshal would no longer feel dead inside, during the fight.

The backswing in Smyth's untrained punch was far too pronounced. Marshal could have seen the blow coming from as early as yesterday afternoon. But instead of comfortably moving out the way of his opponent's fist he shifted his head so that Smyth's delicate hand struck him on the top of the head. Marshal heard the distinct sound of bones cracking.

Not even the cocaine could numb the pain. The imperious plutocrat let out an animalistic howl of agony. The ululation was abruptly cut short by Marshal delivering a left jab and then scything right hook. He deliberately aimed for his opponent's nose and cheek, to prevent his hands being injured by his combatant's bleached teeth. Smyth fell to the floor.

Hunte and Masters gawped on in stunned silence, like goldfish with their mouths permanently open, and were slow to react. But Marshal wasn't. He had no desire to stop and admire his handiwork, as much as the sight of Smyth groaning on the floor, with his nose broken and hair far from styled, was a welcome one. He grabbed the nearest chair and launched it at Masters. The American did and didn't know what hit him. The metal stanchion of the chair struck him just above the eye and broke the skin. A rivulet of blood streamed down his cheek like a tear. The chair also slammed against his elbow. An injury to the funny bone is no laughing matter.

The handsome venture capitalist, a Harvard graduate from Long Island, was more concerned about the state of his looks than the fate of his friends. Brad, when he felt the smart of pain and witnessed the blood on his fingers, retreated inside. He fervently craved a mirror to assess any damage. He had terrifying visions of being disfigured. Masters no longer did any business with Smyth either. The contract between their companies had expired.

Gareth Hunte decided to remain loyal to his friend, however. Hunte, the heir to a sanitary towel empire, had boxed for Oxford and brawled for his rugby club. He had also recently taken part in an Ultimate Fight Club event in the City, which he had won. Hunte adjusted his stance and held his hands up, approaching Marshal like a determined middle-weight coming out of his corner, sniffing in derision or from the cocaine.

For a moment, Marshal remembered his own time in the ring, milling. The contest involved two soldiers pummelling each other, wearing headguards and 18oz boxing gloves, for a minute (or more). "You must aim to dominate your opponent with straight punches to the head," the rules stated. Hands would fly and flail. Attack was the only form of defence. "No ducking, parrying or other boxing defence moves are allowed." It was gladiatorial, adrenaline-fuelled. Brutal. Barbaric. Transcendent. The exercise taught recruits "to deliver maximum violence onto their opponent," – to replicate military combat in microcosm. Marshal, as an officer, didn't need to volunteer to take part in as many bouts as he did. It was a trial by fire. Or Marshal considered it a form of penance. If life could be beaten out of you, why not your sins also? There were times when his face was mottled in bruises. He was a walking Rorschach test. He deserved to suffer. But others deserved to suffer too. Marshal would often arrange matters so that he was paired with the bullies in the squad. God knows whether he was atoning for his sins or not. But he fought like an avenging angel. Busted lips were a better penance than prayer, surely? Marshal flirted with the idea of letting his squat, powerful opponent strike him. Give him a free shot. The Para wanted to know if he could still take a punch. He wanted to pay a debt for his sins. But then he considered that only a good man should meter out any such punishment.

The former Eton prefect thought they might be fighting by Marquess of Queensbury rules. But Marshal harboured no such thought. He first grabbed a wine cooler and threw it at Hunte's square head. He followed up the attack by burying his foot in his opponent's groin. The Para then clasped the Made in Chelsea hopeful by the head – as if he were a priest about to kiss or bless a congregant – and kneed him in the face. His nose burst like a water balloon.

The fight had lasted a minute or so, although most of the participants would feel the effects of the contest for days.

Marshal half-smiled at the waitress, attempting to reassure her. He appreciated how she could easily feel more scared of him now, than any of the well-spoken cretins who had harassed her. He felt a little awkward, although that didn't mean he felt ashamed of his actions. Marshal asked the aghast stranger, who had been standing apart, smoking, to escort the girl back inside.

Marshal followed them in and went to the lavatory. He splashed his face with cold water and took a couple of deep breaths. He calmly exhaled, as if extirpating any unpleasantness. Soon after, his heartbeat returned to normal levels. Would there be dire consequences to his actions? He couldn't care less what his host thought of him, especially after he had witnessed Simon Yale snorting a line of coke whilst feeling up one of his younger guests. Marshal had also acted in self-defence. Unbeknownst to him, Aaron Smyth had no intention of reporting the assault to the authorities. Not only was his pride, as well as body, bruised – but an investigation might lead to a sexual harassment charge. His company could use a legal suit as a justification to terminate his contract, as the trader had failed to hit his targets this year.

17.

Marshal returned to the party. He no longer craved a drink or cigarette when he spotted Grace across the crowded room. They shared a conspiratorial glance. No one else mattered in the room. Grace had recently done the rounds, being introduced to potential suitors or "interesting people" by her friend. Among others, she had met Christian Cable, "a dot com millionaire". Cable had founded a dating app, *The Golden Shot*, which was a cross between *Tinder* and *Elite Singles*. He was forever being profiled in business magazines and was renowned for dating famous models, actresses and reality TV stars. The entrepreneur was fond of trumpeting how he was "self-made". The self-centred Cable, whose idol was Richard Branson, was about to be unmade, however, according to an article Grace had read the week before. Due to suspicious accounting irregularities his investors, including Cable's parents, were about to pull their funding.

"New York's loss is London's gain," Christian exclaimed, as his predatory eyes undressed the model. "I am having a party at my new Battersea apartment next month. You must come along. I can introduce you to the best society in the capital, as a welcome home present."

Grace thanked Cable for the invite, whilst remaining resolutely non-committal. She smiled, but not at the tech millionaire. Rather she recalled a quote, from Byron, which Marshal had mentioned earlier.

"Society is now one polish'd horde/ Form'd of two mighty tribes, the Bores and the Bored," he casually remarked. "Unfortunately, the former turned me into the latter."

Olivia also wanted to introduce the highly prized model to the actor, Hector Stowe. If Grace chose to attend a premiere with the closet homosexual, he would owe the publicist a favour in return. Olivia billed Stowe to Grace as being "the next Eddie Redmayne." Grace duly felt that she now knew enough about the actor to not want to know any more. Especially since she had just found Marshal again.

"Would you like to leave now and have a quiet drink back at the hotel?" Grace asked, after the couple made a beeline for one another.

"No, I would *love* to leave now and have a quiet drink back at the hotel."

The car gunned its way through the countryside. Although swathed in darkness Marshal could still discern the feminine contours of the fields and outlines of the hedgerows and trees, which looked like clumps of broccoli. His mind painted in the greens and autumnal russets and browns, to give the scene some vibrancy and colour.

He drank in her perfume and timeless beauty. Grace sat next to him. She hadn't felt the need to invent an excuse to sit in the passenger seat. Her complexion glowed in the moonlight. Marshal envied her dress, for the way it wrapped itself around her figure and caressed her skin.

Marshal remembered an occasion in the past, when another female client had sat in the passenger seat. The recent divorcee had placed her hand on his thigh, and other parts of his body, while he was driving. It was not the subtlest indicator of interest he had ever received. There was a gear change in their relationship, to say the least. Marshal wanted a similar change in his relations with Grace. But his promise to Porter acted like chocks next to his wheels. Was he being too honourable? But a promise is a promise. It needed to be as strong as a mathematical truth. Stronger. The officer tried not to give his word too much, as he kept it. An oath, for the Catholic, was something sacred. In a world largely devoid of anything sacred, an oath should be sacrosanct. A sense of honour may be proof of the divine, or a manifestation of it. His mother and grandfather always said that he should be a man of his word. Without honour, Man may be no better than a beast, atheist or George Osborne.

Grace gazed out the window. The breeze cooled her flushed skin. The world was a blur. Only Marshal remained sharply in focus. She thought about what might happen back at the hotel. What she wanted to happen. And what would happen?

The hotel bar looked over a croquet lawn. Their drink together was enjoyable, but initially sedate and anti-climactic. Grace initially probed, but Marshal parried. Grace showed plenty of indicators of interest, but Marshal didn't. Perhaps he thought it was not worth investing in their friendship, sharing himself, if their contact with each other was about to end. They still laughed together, however. And there was still hope that she would see him again.

"You will still come to the launch party?"

"Yes. I promise."

Towards the end of the evening, they got talking to an elderly couple, Bob and Lily Arnold, who were celebrating their ruby wedding anniversary. Marshal bought them a bottle of champagne.

"What's your secret?" Grace asked, in relation to staying happily married.

"Not to have any secrets," Bob replied. "And if one person cooks, the other washes up."

"And to be serious about not taking things too seriously," Lily added, smiling with fondness and wisdom.

Bob and Lily mistook the young people for being a couple. Marshal and Grace didn't correct them.

"I see the way she looks at you," Lily remarked to Marshal. "There's a spark there. Or something more than a spark."

Grace beamed, bashfully, and lowered her head, hoping that her hair would cover her blushes.

Shortly afterwards, Marshal and Bob went outside to smoke. The latter lit up a pipe. Marshal liked the smell of the aromatic tobacco. He thought about buying his own pipe when he returned to London. It could be something new in his life.

"You've got a nice lass there," the former postman from Harrogate said, sagely. "My advice is that you stay faithful. It means you love her. And in loving her, you will love yourself more and be content. Trust me."

At the same time, inside, Lily spoke to Grace:

"He's a good man. He dotes on you, it's as plain as day. He's a keeper."

"I know."

The bar closed. Grace kindly invited the elderly couple to the launch event at the bookshop, offering to put them up at a hotel as an anniversary present. The couple were worth ten of the guests she had encountered at the party that night.

Marshal and Grace finally walked upstairs, after talking intimately for another hour. She was tempted to invite him for a nightcap in her room. But she sensed he might decline – and there would be no way back for their friendship as a result. She considered that he might be seeing someone, back in London, and he was being faithful to her – which would only make her more attracted to him.

"I hope you didn't mind being the future Mrs Marshal this evening," he said, playfully.

"There are worse fates," Grace replied, with something more than playfulness in her tone.

Marshal worked through part of the mini-bar in his room. It was too late, he was too tired, to open his laptop and review his files, develop his intelligence picture and plan. He lay awake in bed. The mattress was too soft. The curtains hadn't been pulled across. The amber streetlamp cut an ingot of light across the room. Marshal realised he was half in darkness, half in the light.

He knew his focus needed to be on Baruti. He knew he should have been making plans for his return. But he couldn't stop picturing Grace. She hung in his mind like a stained-glass window in a church. He wrestled with whether she could make him stronger or weaker. Would she let him in if he knocked on her door? He wanted to unzip her dress, feel her skin against his. But he felt like a character from Greek myth, cursed by the Gods. He couldn't break his promise, as much as he wanted to. Who would know, however, if he transgressed? Porter would eventually know and think less of him. But, more importantly, he would know. God would know.

Marshal reasoned however that if he had given his word not to enter the next room – and then discovered that Baruti was sleeping there – he would break his promise, quicker than a politician, and put two in the Albanian's chest and one in his head.

Grace lay awake too, thinking about Marshal. A slight whistle, akin to a kettle boiling, filled the air as the breeze slipped through a gap in the window. Grace believed Marshal to be strong, that he could keep her safe. But she also believed he had a tender side. The world was a lonely, indifferent place on this side of her hotel room wall. But it could be a better, warmer world on the other side of the wall. *With him.* Grace hadn't given herself, her body or her heart, since that night in the hotel with Royce. But she was willing to give both now. Electricity crackled between her ears. Desire, and something else, throbbed within her chest, like a woman locked in an attic trying to get out. She believed Marshal was as lonely and melancholy as she was. They could be better, happier, together rather than apart. Even if they could just be friends. She wanted to hear his dry, wistful voice. She wanted to hear his laugh. He had made her laugh more in two days than others had in two months.

Grace liked the way her feet felt on the cold, tiled floor as she came out of her room and padded along the corridor. The butterflies in her stomach were now doing loop-the-loops. She was wearing sky blue silk pyjamas, with *Fleur of England* lingerie on underneath. Grace told herself that it wasn't just the champagne emboldening her.

She came to his door. Her heart beat alternately with dread and excitement, like two hammers banging away at a breaker's yard. What would she say to him? She hoped that the sight of her would say enough. She tried to catch her breath. Her hand began to tremble, as she lifted it in preparation to knock. What would he say? What if he explained that he was already seeing someone? He might think less of her – and never speak to her again. The model had frequently been accused of stealing boyfriends, or husbands. But the boyfriends and husbands claimed they were single or separated. Yet still, she was blamed for being a homewrecker. Most of the scathing comments came from fellow models or gossip columnists.

Women seldom trust, or like, other women. Grace wondered if Marshal had read any prejudiced or misleading stories about her on the internet.

I don't want to lose him as a friend.

Grace pulled her hand back from the door, like a hand drawing away from a flame, and retreated to her room. She took a couple of sleeping pills (which had been prescribed after her night with Winston Royce). She didn't want to think about Marshal any more. Or anything else. Grace just wanted to be dead to the world.

18.

The mood was subdued during the drive back to Windsor. There was something peculiar, or strained, in the air. Not love, but not indifference either. Grace sat in the front, but she no longer tapped her foot to the music. She typed away on her tablet, jabbing her finger like a pontificating union leader. She was in no mood to take any calls and switched her phone to revert to voicemail. After catching up on some work, Grace rested her head against the window and caught up on some sleep.

Marshal seldom glanced at the model. His focus was on the road – and Baruti. He began to compile a list of preferred locations, should he have to confront the Albanian. Torture and kill him. There were plenty of blind spots and quiet corners in the capital still, if you knew where to look. There was a potential decision to make, whether to ambush Baruti on his own turf, or lure his quarry away into a trap. All the items, which formed part of his plan, had now been delivered to his neighbour. He resolved to book in time at the Marylebone Rifle and Pistol Club. He needed to get his eye in again. The soldier was hoping that any recoil from a gun would jolt him back to life. Marshal would reconnoitre the homes of Baruti and Rugova, as well as their club, *The High Life*. He needed more than just photographs and maps. Marshal also ruminated on the best way he could obtain a sniper's rifle. Ideally, he needed a weapon he was familiar with. An L115A3.

Marshal knew he might have to make haste slowly. Patience is a virtue. He remembered one of his kills in Helmand, at a village close to one of their forward bases. A firefight had broken out. One of his squaddies had been shot and transported out. The enemy scattered like ants. Marshal helped hunt the Afghanis down, street by street. He believed that two Taliban fighters had retreated down a narrow alley and were taking cover in a doorway. The officer set himself up in an elevated position, so he had line of sight along the alley. He didn't want to send any of his unit down the alley, lest the enemy broke cover and fired upon them. And so, he waited. And waited. Hour upon hour. The heat wasn't quite unbearable, because he endured it. Sweat ran down his face like beads of water running down a frosted bottle of beer. He suffered a cramp in his leg – but ignored it. He kept the stock of his rifle nestled in his shoulder, picturing his targets. He kept his sight directed at the space where he believed the enemy would appear. And so, he waited. Stone-like. Stoical. A certain as death. He was given orders to exfiltrate. He declined to respond. The light was fading. Perhaps it was because the two Taliban believed the British had retreated that they broke cover. Marshal scythed them both down. The kills had been worth the wait.

During a meeting with a psychologist, after the incident, Marshal was asked about his first thoughts, after killing the young men. The officer replied that, having witnessed the smoke pouring out the wounds in their chests, he craved a cigarette.

"You seem pleased that two men died," the bespectacled, leftist psychologist commented.

"I was pleased with my marksmanship. But no, I wasn't pleased that I had killed two of the enemy," Marshal replied, lying.

The only good Taliban is a dead Taliban. And the only good Albanian gangster is a dead one, the soldier considered, as he turned off to grab a coffee and scone at a service station. Marshal also thought how he was willing to set up another sniper's nest to wait and take out Baruti and Rugova.

September remained summery. A cordial, honeyed sun warmed the air. The trees had yet to shed all their leaves. Oliver, Victoria and Violet came out to greet Grace and Marshal. Victoria sensed something was slightly awry with her niece and she took her inside for a cup of tea.

"How was the party last night?" Porter asked Marshal, as the latter began to gather his possessions from the guesthouse.

"It was a knockout."

"Will you be able to stay for some lunch?"

Part of Marshal, perhaps more than half, wanted to say yes. He was hungry. He wanted to spend more time with Grace – and Violet.

"No, I'd better get back I'm afraid. I'd like to avoid any traffic."

"Are you sure? You know you're welcome to stay for a few days. I could show you my lack of prowess as a fisherman. I've also got a fine bottle of brandy with your name on it, as well as Napoleon's."

"I'm grateful to you Oliver. But I've got some business to take care of, back in London," Marshal said, picking up the aluminium case which contained the Glock 21.

"You know that you're chasing windmills, James? And I cannot be your Sancho Panza. You won't be able to take them all on. What's your mission here?"

"I just need to take two of them on. What's my mission? To keep drugs off my street. Just my street. I've no ambition to take on the world because I don't much care for the world. I'm no Napoleon. I have no wish to fight my Austerlitz or become Emperor. I'm not looking for some Josephine," Marshal explained.

I'm just looking for some Grace.

"No, but you are looking for trouble. I've seen this before. I had an associate – friend – Michael Devlin. Like you, he was a former Para. He thought that to find some peace, he needed to go to war. Life shouldn't be a crusade. Out of a warped sense of justice, or honour, he took on one job too many. Things will unravel if you fire off too many shots. One round will inevitably go astray – no matter how accomplished a marksman you are."

Porter's expression grew uncharacteristically pained as he thought about Devlin. The person who was worth saving couldn't be saved.

Violet's ears pricked up on hearing her former master's name and she emitted a small whimper.

"I'm not Michael Devlin," Marshal asserted, putting the gun case in his bag. His phone vibrated, with an email reply from the Marylebone Rifle and Pistol Club. He declined to mention that he had once met Devlin.

"Michael had a code. It helped to turn him into an outstanding soldier. But it also helped turn him into a corpse too. He made a promise to his late wife that kept him lonely. I often think to myself I could have somehow intervened. There is no such thing as fate. Or perhaps there is. The older I get, the more I realise how little I know. And that I can't fix everything. But I know that, sooner or later, no good will come from you taking the law into your own hands. People are always asking me for a favour. But I would like to ask you a favour, James. Walk away from this, while you still can. I could still arrange for you to leave the country. Or I could also ask Grace if she still could use a driver. I can pay you. Victoria says that Grace has grown fond of you. You may have grown fond of her too. I'd even be happy to release you from your promise."

"I still have to get back," Marshal steadfastly remarked. He was anxious to leave. Force the issue. He feared that if he stayed another hour, he might end up staying another week or more. Grace couldn't be Calypso and prevent him from returning to the capital. For all of London's dark, satanic mills it was still home.

Marshal zipped-up his jacket in his suit bag. He wondered if it was the most suitable garment to conceal his shoulder holster and Glock. He also wondered whether the inside pocket was deep enough to carry his suppressor.

Porter gazed, or frowned, disapprovingly at a penny-sized fleck of mud on the toe of his polished shoe.

"Out, damned spot," he murmured, as he retrieved a handkerchief and wiped away the offending stain. Porter then frowned disapprovingly at the besmirched white handkerchief.

Grace and Marshal offered each other suitable pleasantries after he put his bags in the boot of the Jaguar. They offered one another fonder and more meaningful looks, when they couldn't be seen by each other. Marshal promised once more that he would see Grace at the launch of the bookshop. She didn't put much stock in his word, however. Men lie, as sure as night follows day. Marshal considered how Grace would have secured a glamorous suitor by the time of the party. Or she might be too busy with her new home and business to spare any time for him. He would still attend the party, as he had given his word, even if it was for five minutes.

Ships that pass in the night.

Fair weather always comes to an end. A murky slab of cloud tiled the horizon, as if a gargantuan foot were about to stamp on the earth. Rain fell like shotgun pellets, in a flash shower, as Marshal drove along the motorway. Lightning licked the sky behind him and then in front of him. The baritone thunder drowned out the sound of the music in the car. But Marshal turned up the volume, as defiant as a Spartan.

Foul weather comes to an end too, though it may not always seem that way. The storm abated, as Marshal came into the capital. He drove through Hammersmith, Earl's Court, Victoria, Vauxhall. London has everything and nothing to offer. It's shiny, yet soulless, he lamented. The streets were not paved with gold, but some may be studded with zircon. There was so much to sigh about. The wind seemed to moan in sympathy. He felt bereft, but not altogether unbowed. Like normal. He thought about the Albanians and his knuckles grew white, like teeth, as he tightly gripped the steering wheel. He chewed the skin on the inside of his cheek. But the welcome sound of the pupils laughing and playing at the school gave him heart. He'd soon be back in his flat, cradling a cigarette and whisky tumbler. Marshal nodded to a couple of neighbours as he retrieved his bags from the boot of the car. He was conscious of keeping an eye out for anyone suspicious, who might observe him entering his block. He didn't see anyone.

But they saw him.

19.

Bisha and Bashkim had turned around the corner, in a bottle-green Toyota with tinted windows, just as Marshal was entering his block. His attention was focussed on pulling the wheels of his travel case up the step. Bishka only caught a glimpse of the Englishman, but a glimpse was all he needed of the man who had hung in his mind's eye over the past couple of days like a wanted poster. The skeevy Albanian's pulse quickened and his nose twitched, like a rat smelling food. He bared his teeth, like a Jack Russell about to attack. But Bisha's desire to take matters into his own hands and confront the Englishman was checked by his fear of Baruti. As much as he had inwardly cursed the kryetar's name over the past couple of days, for ordering him to endlessly drive around the streets of the area, his strategy had reaped the necessary rewards. As usual, Baruti had been right. Bashkim grunted on spying the Englishman, his cheeks swollen from munching on a chicken tikka wrap.

Bisha immediately sent a text message to his superior:

"We found him. He lives on the street where he attacked us."

A message came back, as quick as a counter-punch.

"I know where you are. Do not engage. Just keep watch, from a distance. Even if he sees you, do not approach the target. I will be with you soon."

The Albanian was sitting at a table in *The High Life*. Viktor Baruti permitted himself a smile, as he finished his plate of carpaccio beef and dabbed the corner of his mouth with a linen napkin. A wave of pleasure, almost sexual, rippled through him. They'd found the Englishman. His fate was sealed.

But what should be his fate? The Albanian felt like a gourmet, with an a la carte menu placed in front of him. He had the power to pardon or punish the stranger, who had transgressed. Baruti recalled the fate of Sean Dyke, a

Glaswegian restauranteur and drug dealer who had tortured and murdered one of Baruti's lieutenants. Dyke had first beaten the young Albanian, with a rolling pin, before pouring hot chip fat over his face. In retribution, Baruti found an abandoned warehouse – at which to beat Dyke with a mallet, breaking his kneecaps and several ribs. Baruti watched, without wincing, as the hot chip fat melted his victim's skin. The Scotsman writhed in agony so much he nearly ripped out one of the arms of the chair he was tied to. The hissing sound resembled a gas leak. His eyeballs sizzled. His face looked like something out of a horror movie. The smell was unwholesome and unholy. Putrid. The gruesome screams didn't last too long as Dyke lost consciousness. Baruti's intention had been to torture the Glaswegian for longer, but he had a meeting to attend. So, he put a bullet in his enemy's head, to put him out of his misery. Before commencing to torture Dyke, however, Baruti forced him to watch as his twenty-year-old son was beaten and disfigured in the same fashion he would be. The Albanian considered whether the Englishman should suffer similar justice. An eye for an eye. They could abduct the stranger and meter out the same injuries that he had inflicted upon Bishka and Bashkim. Baruti wondered if the Englishman had a son or brother he could abduct. Lessons must be learned. Something would be wrong with the world, like cutlery placed at an angle, if the call for justice remained unanswered. Baruti received a further text message from Bisha, mentioning that their target had been carrying a travel suitcase. It appeared he had been away on a trip, perhaps with a girlfriend. Baruti was not averse to finding and capturing her. Punishing her. Executing her.

But the Albanian would reserve judgement for now. He wanted to assess the threat of the Englishman first. Was he working alone? What was the extent of his training and contacts? Could he be recruited? Baruti decided to hold off informing his krye about having located their mystery man. He wanted to provide firm intelligence, rather than speculate.

The enforcer was usually loath not to finish a meal, but he cancelled his tiramisu dessert and left his coffee half drunk.

Baruti did not want to waste any more time in confronting the Englishman. He checked the location of Bisha and Bashkim on the app on his phone. They were still on Iliffe Street. His intention was to just talk with the Englishman, but as Baruti got up from the table he drew his pistol and chambered a round. Just in case.

Marshal poured himself a large vodka and lemonade, with crushed ice, when he returned home. He slumped onto the sofa and slept. He was woken by the noise coming from Crampton school as parents collected their children. Marshal felt a sudden urge to check his phone after stirring, hoping to find a message from Grace.

"Hello stranger," the text said. But it was from Tamara.

Marshal didn't reply. He knew that he would always be a stranger to the estate agent, even if he spent a lifetime with her. But it wouldn't be like that with Grace, he realised. He had been a lapsed boyfriend, as well as lapsed Catholic, over the years. He couldn't give himself, even if he had anything to give. But he wouldn't be like that with Grace. Yet Marshal was tempted to contact the fun, attractive woman reaching out to him. She could help him forget about Grace and the Albanians, help him fight off boredom. Dinner, with sex for dessert, would prove enjoyable. But, ultimately, Tamara would be a cause rather than a solution to his boredom.

He thought about the way Grace's glossy hair brushed against her smooth, supple shoulders. The adorable way she wrinkled her nose when she laughed. When she read a book, her eyebrows would subtly shift, becoming more articulate than most people with a wide vocabulary. Marshal thought how his mother would have approved of Grace. She would say that she was kind. He wryly smiled to himself, as he recalled the previous evening. Not the party, but their drinks with Bob and Lily Arnold. He didn't have to pretend too much to play the part of the enamoured fiancé, he realised.

"How did you meet?" Lily asked Marshal. He took a sip of his drink and replied:

"I was staying with some friends. Grace was flying in from New York and she had arranged to stay at the house too. I was walking across the garden when her car pulled up. She was wearing jeans, white pumps and a purple top. She wore her hair down. I remember the scene like it was yesterday, or the day before. I'm not sure how much she even noticed me. Certainly, she had the good sense and taste not to like me. But we spent some time together and gave each other the benefit of the doubt. And God knows how many doubts she must have had about me."

"He conducted a war of attrition," Grace enjoined. "Which, thankfully, he won. He kept making me laugh, being decent and quoting poetry. I did my best not to like him, but fortunately, my best wasn't good enough."

Her eyes were lit up, like muzzle flashes, with humour and something else as she spoke. They shared a look – moment – which only deepened Bob and Lily's belief that the couple were smitten with one another.

He showered. Marshal closed his eyes and imagined the hot water burning away his second skin, so all that was left was just the hardened soldier beneath. Yet all that seemed to be left was a longing for Grace. He turned the tap to allow the cold water to numb him. Numb the longing.

When he finished showering, Marshal attended to his online purchases, picking them up from his neighbour, and turned on the television. Watching the news, listening to detestable politicians pretend to care about a vainglorious world, was akin to eating dead sea fruit. Nothing nourished him. He turned it off. *"Nothing exists except atoms and empty space; everything else is opinion."* But was Democritus not just spouting an opinion? Life could be more than just a collection of atoms and empty space. Faith could be real, as sure as night follows day.

Life could be God, love and Grace. Could be. Should be... We are where we are.

Marshal needed some air. And a drink. He decided to head down to the local pub, *The Manor of Walworth*, which had a beer garden. Whether through forgetfulness or choice he left his gun at home. He liked the pub. Even when it first opened, it had a lived-in feel. The wooden floor was slightly uneven. The décor included an old grandfather clock and dusty chandeliers, which wouldn't have looked out of place in the nineteen seventies. A photograph of the Queen hung by the bar. He wasn't sure whether the pictures had been acquired as a job lot, or specially selected, but portraits of Admiral Cochrane, Palmerston and Christina Rossetti decorated the walls. They sold *Courvoisier* and bacon flavoured *Taytos* crisps. They hosted a monthly pub quiz – which Marshal had won on his own on more than one occasion.

Bishka and Bashkim followed the Englishman on foot. The noose was closing around his neck. Each carried a blade, tucked inside the back of their tracksuit bottoms. Their blood was up, like hounds who had locked onto a scent. The Albanians didn't have to follow the stranger far. Within a few minutes, they watched as Marshal entered the public house. Thankfully, the building had only one entrance/exit. Bishka sent a message to Baruti to update the kryetar on his location.

Baruti ordered an associate to drive him to *The Manor of Walworth*. He was familiar enough with the area to know that there was a police station located around the corner from the venue. The driver searched in vain for a parking space. Baruti thought about who he could pay in the Albanian Government to secure a set of diplomatic plates. The bribe would be costly, but worth it. Timesaving.

He got out of the car on the Walworth Road. The enforcer adjusted his cuffs and swept his hair back. He felt more excited than nervous, in relation to meeting the Englishman – like a teen about to experience a blind date. The encounter could go a variety of ways, he conceded. From killing the vigilante, to offering him employment.

Baruti first met with Bishka and Bashkim. They were sitting on a bench across the road from the pub, half concealed behind a bus stop. He stood over them, with his back to the sun. They squinted as they looked up at their superior. His expression was neutral, inscrutable. As hard as obsidian.

"The kafir is still in there," Bishka remarked, disdainfully. Not that the Albanian had ever been a devout Muslim. He loved beer, pork – and the last time he had visited a mosque he had been suffering from teenage acne. The Albanian could also quote more lines from the *Fast and the Furious* movies than he could from the Koran. "He's dressed in jeans, a polo shirt and white trainers."

"I'll find him. You can remain here. I am just intending to talk to him. I will text you when to bring the car around," Baruti said, his voice staccato. Bullet-like.

The black-clad enforcer walked across the road in a smooth and purposeful gait, like a sheriff about to enter a tavern and eject the town drunk. His gun knocked gently against his ribs, beneath his suit jacket. The coins in his pocket clinked against his housekeys, resembling the sound of spurs.

20.

Baruti spied Marshal through the window. He was sitting out in the beer garden, alone, with a pint in front of him. The Albanian ordered a black coffee. He quickly surveyed the scene. For CCTV (which there wasn't any), entrances/exits and any possible associates of his target. His senses were on high alert. His body was cocked, like a trigger.

A ruddy-faced drunk was standing at the bar. The bags under his eyes were so large that they could have carried the empties from the night before. A crumpled copy of *The Racing Post* sat in front of him, along with a betting slip with three names scrawled on it: *Fountain Pen Blues*, *Comus*, *Ambushed*. He thought the latter was an omen. Not that he believed in omens. The only higher power in Viktor Baruti's life was Viktor Baruti. An old soldier, wearing some service medals on his jacket, having come from a memorial dinner, sat in another corner, with a ten-thousand-yard stare on his crinkled face. Without fuss or fanfare, the former Para had paid for a couple of drinks to be left in the pump for the veteran, when he entered earlier.

Marshal stretched his arms out and arched his back. His neck muscles were wound tighter than a Scottish Jew, or anyone who would take offence at such a comment, the soldier joked to himself. Marshal let the sun massage him, melt away the icy knots beneath his skin. The wound in his shoulder began to throb too, conscious that he hadn't felt a single twinge or tightening during his time away from London.

He sat at a one-piece wooden bench and table set on the grass. Half a dozen other tables sat either side of a concrete path. A few sparrows darted overhead, their birdsong often drowned out by the sound of trains clattering across a bridge, which ran along the back of the pub. But the scene was still peaceful, restorative.

For some reason, his thoughts turned to Michael Devlin. His story was shrouded in mystery. Not even Porter had been able to entirely understand him. Marshal had met Devlin at a charity event one evening, many years ago. They peeled away from the party to smoke a cigarette. Marshal liked the former squaddie. He had an unapologetic dry sense of humour. They spoke about their time in Helmand (they were at first guarded but then candid about their activities there). They also spoke about their favourite Graham Greene novels and the anti-climax of civilian life. "The term may be an oxymoron," Marshal joked. Devlin was still married back then. Happily married, he asserted.

"I know, I used to think being happily married was a paradox too," Devlin added. "I was lucky. I met the right woman."

"How do you know when you've met the right woman?" Marshal asked, believing that the date he had brought to the event was the wrong woman.

"You just know," he replied, content rather than self-satisfied.

Marshal had dismissed Devlin's words. Until now. He closed his eyes and pictured Grace. Elated. Uplifted. He had checked his phone, more than once, hoping to see a message from her. Marshal half-smiled more than once as he remembered noticing a well-thumbed paperback copy of *The End of the Affair* poking out of her handbag. *I think I'm in love*, Marshal had thought to himself. But this time, he wasn't joking. Grace wasn't Calypso. She was Penelope.

It was time to make a leap of faith and contact her, he decided. *Ask her out to dinner.* Today would be the first day of the rest of his life, should she say yes. He pulled out his phone.

Footsteps sounded on the metal stairway which led down to the beer garden. Marshal glanced up and put his phone away.

Baruti.

They'd found him. It was potentially game over. Marshal did his utmost to suppress any flicker of recognition. But inside his heart sank, as if he had just been diagnosed with cancer. He buried his face in his pint glass to hide his expression.

Marshal felt like it was only the starch in his shirt holding him up. Part of him was tempted to run. He recalled the NCA files about Baruti entering establishments in Glasgow – and attacking or executing his enemies. Was he here to kill him? Marshal no longer pictured Grace, as if her image was formed in sand and the Albanian had blasted it away. His war may have been over, before it had a chance to start. Half his tactical advantage derived from his anonymity, invisibility.

Marshal took in the Albanian, as he walked towards him. He was unlikely to pull his gun, balancing his coffee cup, with no expedient escape route. With a police station around the corner and CCTV cameras littered along the main road outside. His eyes were bluer than the photographs suggested, the colour of a blowtorch flame. His suit was as black as the grim reaper's garb, his features as sharp as a katana. Marshal also fancied that, should Baruti had been a little paler and gaunter, he would have resembled a vampire. He was somehow underwhelmed by the infamous Albanian. The spectre – who had haunted his thoughts and dreams for the past couple of days – had been made flesh. He noticed coffee-stained teeth, a small shaving nick, a frayed cuff and a few grey hairs.

Marshal couldn't afford to lose the remaining part of his tactical advantage. The enemy was still unaware of the intelligence he had gathered. He needed to bluff, lie. Thankfully, life was mostly about bluffing, to oneself and others. Life was a game of poker. People told themselves every day that they were good, honest souls. That they would do anything – absolutely anything – for the sake of their children, aside from stay married and remain faithful. That there wasn't a racist bone in their bodies, as they moved out of Hackney so they could send their children to a school in Saffron Walden. That they voted against Brexit because they were outward-looking, progressive, lovelier than those who voted for it.

They locked eyes. Neither exhibited any animus. Marshal stared at the Albanian as if he were a complete stranger.

"Do you mind if I sit here?" Baruti politely, yet firmly, asked.

"That's fine," Marshal replied, confounded. Dumbfounded. Playing a part.

"You do not know who I am. But I have you at a slight advantage. I know a little about you. I know where you live. I know you had an altercation with a couple of my employees a few days ago," the Albanian said, stirring his coffee four times and tapping his spoon against the cup twice.

Marshal finally offered a flicker of recognition and pretended that the penny had dropped.

"I remember," he replied, taking a swig of his pint again whilst casually glancing up at the windows of the pub, scanning for any of Baruti's associates. He also took in the potential weapons on the table. Glasses, ashtrays. His hardback copy of *The Power and the Glory* could be slammed into his counterpart's throat. The slim, stainless steel pen he used to complete a crossword could easily be used to stab the Albanian in the eye or temple. But if Baruti was here to kill him, he would be dead already.

"Please, do not worry. I am alone. I am just here to talk," Baruti stated, holding up his hands defensively, non-threateningly, as he sat down. The enforcer wanted to initially put the Englishman at ease. Both killers adopted an equitable tone. "Firstly, can I ask your name? I would ask you to do me the courtesy of telling the truth. Honesty is always the best policy. I will know if you're lying. We now know where you live, on Iliffe Street."

"As much as your employees may consider that my name is mud, you can call me James."

"My name is Dmitri," Viktor remarked, after sipping his coffee. He narrowed his unblinking eyes and scrutinised Marshal, taking in the lines of his jacket to see if he was carrying a weapon. He was surprised to see that the Englishman was still half-smiling. "I take it that you served in the military. Certainly, you are not without some training."

"How do you know I served in the military?"

"Let's just say it takes one to know one," the borderline psychopath remarked. "As much as we be standing on opposites sides of the fence, we probably have plenty of things in common. It may even be the case, after I check your credentials, that I offer you a job within our organisation. Before I can do that, however, I need to know if you are currently working for any of our rivals. Were you paid to attack my men, or are you just some kind of lone, good Samaritan?"

"I'm seldom called a good Samaritan. I could get used to it though. But you now know where I live. I'm not working for any of your rivals. I attacked your men, after I was assaulted by a cigarette butt first, to keep my neighbourhood safe," Marshal explained, reasonably. He was akin to a swan gliding effortlessly, serenely, across the water – as his legs paddled furiously beneath the surface. He cursed his bad luck at having been found. Or was he at fault? If only he had accepted Porter's offer to stay at his house – or go on holiday for a while. Or he could still be with Grace. Retribution from the Albanians could prove swift. They could come for him tonight. Should he just grab his passport and toothbrush and disappear? A tactical retreat might be the order of the day.

The rackety noise of a train passing overhead vexed the Albanian and interrupted him, just as he was about to speak. For a few seconds, he glowered at the train. Baruti looked like he wanted to kill every soul on board. He tapped his foot, impatiently waiting for the sound to subside, before continuing to speak.

"As a soldier, I appreciate that you probably have a code of honour. But you need to understand that we have a code of honour too. There must be honour among thieves, no? Like soldiers serving in a regiment, we need to trust one another, fight for each other. Our code demands we should punish you. By attacking one of us, you attack all of us. You understand?"

"I understand."

The Albanian didn't know whether to be impressed or confused by the half-smile still lining the Englishman's features. He was half-expecting that the stranger would attempt to escape, or assault him, or beg for mercy, when he made himself known to his target. Perhaps the ex-soldier was suffering from some form of trauma. Conflict, violence, was too deeply ingrained in him as a way of life. He wanted to fight – or die.

"You do not appear too worried by this. A smarter man would be afraid. Do you have a death wish?"

"I can't say I'm overly enamoured with life, but I don't believe I have a death wish," Marshal replied, remembering a scrap of conversation he had with Porter a couple of nights ago. The fixer was thinking about Devlin and asked Marshal if he was afraid of dying.

"No, I'm not. I am perhaps scared of having something to live for, however. Because then I might be afraid of dying and losing something precious… If you devalue life enough, death becomes more of a reward than punishment… Death is inevitable. I'd be foolish not to accept it. Maybe, given the unpleasantness of life, it's even worth embracing."

But Marshal had said that before getting to know Grace.

Baruti exhaled and flared his nostrils. He was beginning to grow irritated by the glib Englishman. He wanted to wipe the half-smile off his face. Should he decide to abduct and torture the ex-soldier, he might give him the chance to fight for his life. The Albanian was tempted to test himself against his opponent. It was time to break him.

"You think this is all some kind of a joke? I can say with some confidence that we'll have the last laugh, James. Do you think you will just be able to go to the police? Now there's a real joke. We have policemen on our payroll. We will know what's happening before you do. Your neighbourhood is now our neighbourhood. Should I give the word, your life as you know it will be over. You probably thought yourself some type of vigilante, who was cleaning up the streets? Americans are always accused of watching too many movies. But the English are just as guilty of being deluded. You think you are the cowboy, Shane? That, at the end, some innocent mewling child will call out to you, "You're a good man, Shane." But it's all bullshit. If you are the hero in this story, you're a tragic hero. You must also understand that your death will not be the end of things. You attacked my friends, my family. Therefore, I will find and attack yours."

Baruti's tone was now menacing. He bared his teeth as he spoke – like a vampire baring his fangs.

Marshal pictured Grace. And Oliver and Victoria. He could not return to Windsor, in case he was followed. He couldn't afford to put them in any danger. Or even contact them. Should Grace call or text he would ignore her. It might be best to delete her contact details, until it was safe. He also thought about his father and wondered if he should apprise him of the situation. His guts became knotted. He wanted the ground to swallow him up, as he buried his head in his hands in despair. Marshal felt like surrendering to his fate. What choice did he have? He wouldn't beg for his life, but he would beg for others. If they were playing poker, the Albanian was holding all the aces. If they were playing chess, it would be checkmate.

A chill wind cut through the warm air. A burst of laughter emanated from inside the pub, seemingly mocking him. Should Marshal have been in possession of his gun, he looked like he might shoot himself rather than his enemy.

Baruti grinned, as the half-smile was finally wiped from the Englishman's good-humoured expression. He enjoyed seeing people scared. It amused and nourished his dark psyche. Marshal's bluff demeanour and bravado disappeared. The mask had fallen to the floor, the Albanian judged. The Englishman finally bowed his head, unable to bear Baruti's scorching, interrogative aspect any more. His features were strained, as if he were about to breakdown and cry. Defeated, rather than defiant.

"What do you want from me?" Marshal murmured, his voice cracked. Like his heart. His hand trembled as he picked up his pint and drank from it, hoping to moisten his sawdust-dry throat.

"Nothing, for now. But I will be in touch. I want to run some checks on you first, James. Find out more about you. Paranoia is a virtue, a survival skill, in my business. Something about you doesn't quite add up. But you realise you have a debt to pay. You can either pay it in your blood, or someone else's. I may offer you the opportunity to work off your debt. Of course, your instinct may be to flee. But not all of your family and friends will be able to follow you. We will make them pay off the blood debt, if you are unwilling to do so. You wouldn't want us to break our code, would you? We are men of our word. If we say we will pay someone, we pay someone. If we say we will make a delivery, we will make a delivery. And if we promise to kill someone, we will keep that vow. But do not despair completely. We are also businessmen, willing to make a deal with you. From the manner with which you attacked my employees, it appears you have something to offer us. You have a bloodlust, which we can help you satisfy. Our strength comes not from defeating our rivals – but working with them. At first, the Columbians could do without us, but now they come knocking on our door to sell their product. Once, we were the junior partners of the Italians. But now we work with them, as equals. One day they may even work for us. Peace is more prosperous than war. I would rather have you as an ally than an enemy, James. You may even find that you enjoy paying off your blood debt, by working for us. There are worse fates," Baruti remarked, taking a sip of his coffee, enjoying his moment of triumphant.

Marshal just listened. Took things in. There was little he could say in reply. He was apparently bereft of pithy comebacks. Subdued. Subjugated. The soldier nodded and said he understood his orders. He would not flee. He would not go to the police. He would not interfere with the organisation's business activities in his neighbourhood.

"Can I go now?" Marshal said, like a child asking to be excused from the dinner table.

"Yes. That will be all, for now. I am about to head home shortly. But I will be in touch within the next few days. How did they say it in the movie, Casablanca? *This could be the beginning of a beautiful friendship*," Baruti remarked, with a sly, wolfish grin.

Marshal stood up and walked away, his footsteps as leaden as the clouds on the horizon, his chin sunk into his chest, like a mourner walking to or from a funeral.

21.

Celine Dion played in the background, but thankfully not for too long, as the two women sat in the kitchen. Victoria and Grace were working their way through their second bottle of wine. Porter had made himself scarce, retreating into his study upstairs. He was attempting, with a high degree of failure, to tie a couple of flies in preparation for a fishing trip later in the week.

"I didn't think you liked James at first. I even tried to keep you apart," Victoria remarked.

"I didn't. But then I got to know him. I know it sounds silly, or a cliché, but I miss him already. Perhaps I didn't get to know him enough," Grace replied. Victoria couldn't tell if the wine was fuelling or quelling her niece's distress.

"I should warn you that you may never get to know James properly. He's a soldier. No one quite knows what they're thinking about when they have a thousand-yard stare on their face. God knows how long I've been married to Oliver – but I cannot say that I know him completely. Which doesn't mean that I do not love him."

Grace felt another twinge of regret. She sipped – or more than sipped – her wine. She wasn't so much worried that she hadn't got to know Marshal. But that she would never get to know him. There were moments when she had felt she had been in love – and happy – when she was with him. Grace thought of Turgenev. Love and happiness can exist in this world, but only briefly.

The only love stories are tragic love stories.

"I think we may have lost our moment. It's my own fault."

"You shouldn't be too hard on yourself. Maybe I should be hard on myself though. I have something to confess. I asked Oliver to tell James not to hit on you. I'm sorry, I thought it was for the best. Oliver did tell me today that he thought that James was fond of you though."

"Did Oliver say anything else?"

"As you may have worked out yourself, Oliver often keeps his cards close to his chest. Even his secrets have secrets. He did warn me that there were certain topics that James wouldn't want to discuss, such as his time in the army, and the death of his mother and grandfather. James may be someone who just doesn't give much of himself."

Grace's twinge of regret turned to one of hope. James had given something of himself over the past few days. She remembered him opening up about his mother, with a haunted expression, as they spoke, deep into the night, at the hotel bar.

"I think about her every time I walk past a church. She was a devout Catholic. But all I do is walk by, rather than walk in. I worry that if I walk in and find God then I will experience an unbearable amount of guilt, for the times God – and my mother – prompted me to enter and I ignored them. But what if I walk in and I don't feel anything? What if the hymns ring hollow? What if I take communion and I still feel hungry? If vodka means more to me than the blood of Christ? If I don't hear the call of God or my mother? The world would seem to me even tawdrier – and less than nothing."

"The next time you should walk in, rather than walk by. If you feel you've got nothing, then you may have nothing to lose," Grace advised. The Catholic placed one hand on his, on the table, whilst fingering the cross around her neck. There was a look of grief on his anguished face. He was missing his mother, or God, in his life. Or just someone to love him, she judged.

"I wish I had your faith."

"I wish I had your country music playlist."

Marshal laughed, as they shared another moment.

Grace also listened as the former officer spoke a little about his time in Afghanistan, and his time afterwards. Marshal didn't quite know his place in the world, or whether he wanted to be in the world at all.

"I still feel like I should be a soldier, standing a post. But I no longer know what it is I'm supposed to be fighting for… I did some things in Helmand that I shouldn't be proud of, including being proud of them. There are some sins which shouldn't be forgiven. There are some debts that can't be repaid."

Grace's heart went out to Marshal, which she felt good about – because it proved she still had a heart. Not all men were bastards. Just most of them. Grace listened with sympathy as Marshal revealed how he was still dealing with his grief, in relation to his grandfather.

"We're taught when we're young that we will grow and develop as a person. That society continually improves too, whether we're on some whiggish journey of progress or, God forbid, we're heading towards some leftist, communist promised land. But the only truth is that we're born to die. Society doesn't always progress, especially in the name of "progress". Things decay. My grandfather lost his memories and faculties, like leaves falling from a tree. I did my best by him, but I was swimming against the stream. I miss Teddy every day, but I can't keep grieving. I feel guilty every day. I have to cast out thoughts about him, as though I were casting out evil spirits. But remembering him is just too painful. Even good memories – or especially good memories – hurt. If God created the world then he also built in decay, grief and torment. Rather than praising God for creating an intelligent world, shouldn't we condemn him for creating a cruel one? But I worry I'm being cruel, as opposed to intelligent, by talking too much. I'm in danger of becoming as dull as Jemima Khan or Damien Hurst," Marshal posited. Shortly afterwards she caught him gazing out the window, with a thousand-yard stare.

Her aunt may be wrong, for once. Grace dared to believe that Marshal could give something of himself. He might harbour feelings for her, similar to the ones she harboured for him. If Marshal didn't get in touch with her by the end of the evening, then she would reach out to him tomorrow. All wasn't lost. Grace would ask him out for dinner, as a thank you for him driving her around over the past couple of days. It would be a start.

Grace glanced at her phone, checking to see if Marshal had already messaged her. He hadn't. But she hadn't lost hope.

Viktor Baruti took another sip of his black, treacly coffee. He enjoyed the restorative quiet of the garden, which Marshal had previously taken advantage of. For a time, the Englishman's flippancy had irritated the Albanian. His blood had been close to boiling over. Eventually, he had found his opponent's weak spot – and broke him. The debt would be paid, one way or another. But first, the intelligence officer would run a full background check on the Englishman. It was unlikely he was a plant, by the security services, but he needed to be certain. He was curious to study the soldier's service record – and to know whether he had a criminal record. And if so, what for? The operations officer would assess his skills set. Had he killed before? Baruti was confident that James could prove an asset. He may even one day become a friend. The kryetar smiled into his coffee cup as he considered how the vigilante would soon be working as a criminal. Today could be the first day of the rest of his life.

Baruti did not dwell on his success for too long. There were other fronts to fight on. He made a call to his counterpart, Tristen, in the Hellbanianz. They discussed producing a video, which could be shown via YouTube, in order to attract "falcons" – new recruits. The video would glamorise a life of crime, showing drugs, bikini-clad women, bling, Bentleys and rolls of cash, over a soundtrack of hip-hop music. A previous video, *The Hood Life*, had generated over 7.5 million hits. The gang's Instagram account had over a hundred thousand followers. Baruti was conscious of balancing the need to recruit new blood, particularly teenagers from existing street gangs, without overexposing their organisation.

"I'm like the fucking Pied Piper of London. I put out these videos and lead the dumb bastards into a life of crime. The gangs are even now choosing to work for us over the West Indians, to sell product," the racist Tristen exclaimed. "Even if they stabbed each other at twice the rate we'd still have enough personnel."

Baruti finished his coffee and sent a text to Bisha, instructing him to collect the car and park outside the pub. He worked his way through some WhatsApp messages, issuing orders to dealers and enforcers alike for the evening ahead.

Thirty minutes later he was in the front passenger seat of the vehicle, driving to his flat. The Toyota worked its way along the Old Kent Road, Tower Bridge Road, Jamaica Road, towards Canada Water. He noted a new cocktail bar on Tooley Street. He would have one of his men check the establishment out, for a possible site to sell their product. Rugova mentioned the other day how their organisation needed to increase their investment in – and acquisition of – suitable local businesses.

"We are the gods of the street," some gang members had boasted during one of the recruitment videos. But really, they were minions, and all too mortal. The true gods were Rugova, Tristen and himself. London was the cocaine capital of Europe. They would soon have a stranglehold on South London, in the same manner that the Hellbanianz held sway in East London. People often talked about the war on drugs. But the war was over. The criminals had won.

He caught the smell of weed in the air, wafting through the window. It smelled like money. Baruti glanced around him as they got stuck in traffic near Bermondsey Street. He smiled – his mouth as thin and tight as a tourniquet – as he surveyed the people around him. There were few, true Londoners any more. The working-classes had chosen to move to the suburbs or been driven out by the cost of living in the capital. The area was now awash with hipsters from the home counties, sporting beards, spouting dumb opinions. Uneducated graduates. Keyboard warriors. Young professionals, sponging off their parents. The women wore revealing tops and short skirts. Baruti found their rolls of fat and flesh disgusting. Half of the women complained that they received too much attention from men, the other half complained that they didn't receive enough. Whores! Cigarettes and alcohol had become sins, yet people were godless. Entitlement was rife. They thought that their political parties could solve their problems. They were obsessed with taking pictures of themselves, recording their contemptible lives. They endlessly whined. The sound had become as constant as the wind. The West bred weak, effeminate characters. The Albanian sometimes felt like slashing their self-satisfied faces with a razor. Their one virtue was that they became easily addicted to drugs. Cocaine was killing London. *Let it.* Cocaine wasn't a sin, or a toxin. Cocaine was manna, to its users. Even if they legalised drugs his organisation would still be able to sell a purer product at a more competitive, untaxed price. Let them legalise brothels too. They would still corner the market. Baruti and his organisation would still be the gods of the street. People were zombies, in all sorts of ways. Baruti didn't like the English middle-classes, but he liked the money they spent on his product. It was an irony, which the kryetar was all too conscious of, that the same people he despised, provided him with a living. The joke was on them, however.

Bishka and Bashkim remained silent during the drive. They knew better than to disturb their kryetar while he tapped away on his phone. They didn't dare play any music either. But both men were eager to know how his meeting with the Englishman went. Bashkim had spent more than a fleeting moment imagining their enemy tied to a chair, naked and bloody. He would flick open his cigarette lighter. By the time he finished torturing him, no one would be able to tell where the cuts and bruises ended, and the burn marks began.

"So how did your talk go with the Englishman?" Bishka asked, unable to suppress his curiosity any longer. They were close to Baruti's home, passing by Canada Water tube station and the steel, rhombus-shaped library opposite it.

"It went well. Things are in hand."

"Are we going to pay him a visit?" Bisha replied, licking his lips. Almost panting, like a dog straining on a leash.

"Yes, but not yet. The blood debt will be paid. The Englishman will no longer be a problem."

The light was fading. Iron-grey clouds rolled across the sky overhead, like a German tank division, intent on destruction.

Bishka turned into a cul-de-sac and parked opposite the entrance to Baruti's plush apartment building.

Bashkim sat in the middle of the backseat, checking his "Likes" for the pictures he had taken at the gym last week. Refreshing the page was almost as addictive as the drugs he sold.

As soon as Bishka pulled to a stop he checked his mobile as well. He had a message from Sophia, one of the prostitutes he had met at *The High Life*. The Albanian had texted if she was free to meet. Sophia replied she could meet, but her time wouldn't be free. The escort did offer Bisha a slight discount on her hourly rate, however. He smiled, optimistically and amorously, believing that she might genuinely like him.

Baruti's phone vibrated and chimed. The kryetar didn't recognise the number, but that wasn't unusual. He swiped the screen and answered, his voice devoid of any emotion.

"Viktor speaking."

"If you want peace, prepare for war."

The name of the horse, *Ambushed*, had indeed been an omen. But not in the way he expected. Baruti recognised the quote and voice. He recognised the figure standing in front of the car, even though the Englishman was wearing sunglasses and a baseball cap. The Albanian even recognised the type of pistol pointing at him, a Glock 21, with a suppressor attached. He recognised all these things in an instant, just before the Glock spat out a couple of rounds and everything went black.

Marshal had pulled the trigger twice, seemingly devoid of emotion. The windscreen splintered, without shattering. Blood splattered the glass from the inside as the bullets darted into Baruti's chest. His heart burst, like a watermelon. Marshal didn't dwell on the killing, however. As he needed to kill again. Bishka was targeted next. His hand was steady, his aim was true. The first bullet hissed out the suppressor and shattered the drug dealer's sternum; the second blew away half his throat.

Bashkim's eyes were stapled wide with shock and terror. He tried to move, but the plaster cast on his leg got stuck underneath the front seat. The hulking Albanian swore in his native language, either directing the curse towards the Englishman or the ill-designed car, as the jacketed 44mm round turned his stomach inside out. Blood immediately soaked his white, tight-fitting t-shirt, which he wore beneath a banana-coloured puffer jacket that even a Scouser would have thought too garish. The second bullet painted a Jackson Pollock-type picture against the back windscreen, using what little brains were contained in the enforcer's head.

Marshal had continued to walk, with his head bowed down, until he was out of sight of Bishka and Bashkim, who he spotted across the road as he exited the pub earlier. After he turned off the main road, however, he sped to his flat. Once there he changed his clothes, armed himself with the Glock and picked-up his pre-packed backpack, containing recent online purchases.

The ultimate bluff, lie, to Baruti had been that Marshal was defeated, instead of defiant. A mask hadn't fallen. It had been put on. Marshal convinced his opponent that he was no longer a threat. He particularly liked the touch of making his hand tremble, as he reached for his pint. A blood debt was about to be paid, but not in the way the Albanian envisioned. Baruti made a mistake – a fatal one – in telling Marshal that he was heading home. Marshal had already selected the secluded cul-de-sac, free from CCTV coverage, as a prospective location to ambush his target.

Using a few short-cuts, he reached Canada Water in good time and parked the Jaguar at Surrey Quays shopping centre. Marshal waited in a quiet alley, situated at the end of the cul-de-sac. Baseball cap and sunglasses were donned. He retrieved the hands-free mic and headphones from his bag, as well as put on the latex gloves he had bought. Marshal unsnapped the small leather guard on his shoulder holster, for ease of access to the Glock. His target would come into his sights soon. The ex-Para licked his dry lips and wiped his sweaty palms. *It's good to be scared. It means you're human. Yet fear can be overcome, like an enemy.* Marshal controlled his breathing. His half-smiled returned. It was like he was back in the army again. Carrying a gun. Focussed and purposeful. Killing.

The car pulled into the apartment complex, containing the three Albanians. All his eggs were in one basket. It was unlikely that he would be blessed with such an opportunity again. God was on his side, he half-joked.

Marshal drew the Glock, attached the suppressor and pressed the button on a burner phone to make the call to the Albanian. Not only did he want Baruti to know who had bested him – but with his phone to his ear, the assassin would be unable to retrieve his gun quickly. The devil is in the detail.

The bastards deserved to die.

The smell of cordite was as pungent and familiar as incense. The scene wasn't that of a gunfight, between two cowboys – but rather a slaughter. Execution. Baruti's head lolled to one side. His features were creased in anguish, like someone suffering a nightmare in their sleep. Blood frothed out of Vasil Bisha's mouth, as if he were experiencing a macabre fit. Tarin Bashkim didn't complain too much as his killer unburdened him of the envelope, bulging with cash, in his jacket pocket.

Marshal detached the suppressor and holstered the Glock. He briefly sighed in relief and respite. He half-smiled, partly because the plan he devised was only half complete. Marshal unzipped his backpack and placed the Jamaican flag he purchased over the head of Baruti, like a veil. Both the Albanians and the police would hold Delroy Onslow and the West Indians responsible for the hit. Before taking his leave, Marshal unlocked the boot of the Toyota. Thankfully, he found what he was looking for – several kilos of cocaine, a selection of bladed weapons and half a dozen handguns.

22.

Marshal disposed of the burner phone he used to call Baruti on, before returning to the car. He also collected and destroyed all mobile phones belonging to the Albanians. Should someone from one of the apartments have witnessed or filmed the hit, his hat and sunglasses would ensure that he still wouldn't be recognised. There were no sirens to be heard. The police were probably out investigating a slew of preposterous hate crimes. Maybe a feminist had turned up at a trans-positive seminar at a university, and they needed to create a safe space for the students.

As much as he tried to remain calm and focussed, a torrent of adrenaline coursed through Marshal as he sat in the car and drew breath. He could still feel the recoil of the Glock through his arm. Anxiety and exhilaration competed, like rival warlords, for sovereignty over his mood. The feeling was similar to when he had chalked up his first kill in Helmand. His commanding officer put money behind the bar, to celebrate him losing his virginity. He didn't want his young officer dwelling too much on the incident. "Job done," the Major said, reassuringly. "Better he bought it than you or your men." The drink helped wash away any guilt he might have felt over the mortal sin. It had been a fun night. Songs were sung. The jokes were as filthy as the rubbish bags after the event. Come the morning the officer's head throbbed, as if he had been shot.

Marshal smoked a couple of cigarettes, but still, he felt wired and fidgety. He glanced at his watch. The timepiece had been a gift from the regiment, when he left the army. The *Omega Seamaster* was famed for being the watch of choice of James Bond. Marshal had earned the nickname "Licence to Kill" due to his record in Helmand. His Lance-Corporal had arranged for the watch to be engraved.

"To James. Live and Let Die."

It was approaching 19:00. He was still on schedule. Baruti had been taken off the board.

One down. One to go.

Marshal drove home and changed once more. He drank a finger of whisky and smoked a cigarette, before heading out again. *No rest for the wicked.* He went through the next phase of his plan whilst driving to the target, *The High Life* nightclub. The intelligence files suggested it was highly likely Luka Rugova would be at the venue. He parked the car a couple of streets away.

It was 20:15. A queue was snaking outside the club as Marshal walked past and surveyed the scene. He saw lots of blouses and ripped, skinny jeans – and that was just what the men were wearing. He heard a few snippets of conversation and rolled his eyes, not knowing whether to groan or laugh.

"Mummy said she'd pay for me, so I could concentrate on developing my blog... People don't realise how stressful exams can be. Colleges should be devoting more funding to counsellors... Brexit is evil. I don't know how I'll cope... I cried so much when Bowie died. It was like the world lost a really cool best friend. I still think his best album is probably his Greatest Hits... I read some articles online, as well as some tweets. Churchill was a war criminal..."

A well-dressed Albanian, with good English and a convivial manner, worked his way along the line of nightclubbers and sold product to his regular customers. Plenty of people would be putting shit up their nose during the night. There was plenty of space between their ears to store it all, Marshal considered.

"Got any gear, mate?" one nightclubber said, accosting Marshal, mistaking him for a dealer. The twentysomething wanted to buy rather than sell. Although he was wearing a hoodie and affected a mockney accent he couldn't quite disguise his home counties roots. Marshal suspected he attended Exeter University, being too dim to get into Oxford or Cambridge. He probably worked in digital marketing and had recently switched to drinking soya milk.

Marshal was tempted to break the snowflake's jaw, or at the very least his nose, but he understandably didn't want to draw attention to himself. He merely shook his head and walked on.

Rain began to spot the air and a drizzle followed. But Marshal saw everything clearly through the misty air. He slipped down an alleyway, running behind the club. The scene thankfully resembled the photographs he had scrutinised beforehand. There was a lack of CCTV. The alley was poorly lit, and few people chose to walk down it. The vent was there, with the large, covered bins beneath, which Marshal could stand on. No plan survives first contact with the enemy, the military precept, from Helmuth von Moltke, dictated. Marshal was resolved to immobilise anyone who disturbed him. If necessary, he would kill them. It'd be one less body to occupy a prison cell one day.

Marshal wore a pair of latex gloves again as he climbed onto the bin and, using an electric screwdriver, removed the vent cover. He placed the holdall, containing the drugs, guns and knives, into the hole in the wall and resealed the vent. Finally, cocaine was about to do some good in the world. The amount contained in the plastic bags wouldn't be able to be passed off as being for personal use, even if Keith Richards was in the building. Marshal felt like kissing the bags and wishing them Godspeed in being found and used to prosecute Rugova, but he was mindful of not leaving any trace evidence. He also hoped that the police would be able to use ballistics to match the handguns to various murders, in Glasgow and London.

Marshal adopted a slight Irish accent, when he made the call from another burner phone. His voice was rife with anxiety and fear when he reported how he had just witnessed a couple of men enter *The High Life* nightclub, carrying handguns. He also said he observed another man go around the back of the club with a large, black holdall. When asked by the emergency call handler to give his name Marshal replied that he was too scared to offer it. He wanted to remain anonymous.

Marshal was confident that the call would be flagged-up to Martin Elmwood or a colleague in his unit. And it was.

"Not even David Beckham's lawyer will be able to get you off this time," Elmwood remarked to Luka Rugova, unable or unwilling to disguise the satisfaction he felt, as the Albanian was cuffed in his office.

Rugova forced a smile, or snarled, in response. The cuffs bit into his wrists. His air of calm and confidence finally shattered, He spat out curses, in English and Albanian, at the police officers rummaging through his office as if it were a flea market. They were uninvited guests in his home. Rugova protested that the black holdall they had found, full of weapons and cocaine, had been a plant. He recognised the holdall however and tried to think if he had personally handled any of the bags of cocaine or handguns.

The crime boss threatened Elmwood, whilst being filmed, and assaulted another officer whilst resisting arrest. In the tussle, the bust of Napoleon fell off his desk and smashed on the floor. He also kicked out and put his foot through the plaster wall, near the door. Rugova felt his phone continually vibrate in his pocket, with messages and missed calls, as if the device were experiencing a fit.

Ferid had just been similarly led away, after losing his Buddha-like serenity and resisting arrest. The police took great pleasure in tasering the hulking bodyguard, bringing him down like a bunch of cavemen subduing a woolly mammoth. He was tasered, clubbed and accidentally kicked in the head, twice. Elmwood couldn't quite remember the last time he had enjoyed himself so much.

The raid came shortly after the Albanian received the devastating news that his lieutenant and friend had been murdered. The West Indians were likely responsible, given that their calling card of a Jamaican flag was found at the scene. Before Rugova could fully process his grief and the enormity of the situation the police arrived. He missed his lieutenant more than his friend at that moment – and he cursed their contacts in the police for not forewarning him about the raid, after being unable to reach Viktor. When he paid someone, he expected them to do their job.

When the raid started Rugova tried to call his lawyer, but it went straight to voicemail. Before the raid he had received a message from his girlfriend, Mona, to say she needed help working the new TV. Could he come over? His wife had also called to say their son had been crying, after being responsible for his team losing a key football match. Could he come home early? The gods were conspiring against the Albanian, it seemed. He was worried for his empire, and family – in that order.

He would, at the very least, spend the night in the cells. With Baruti gone, there was no one competent or trustworthy enough to manage things in his absence. He would need to retaliate against the West Indians. Delroy Onslow needed to die – blood for blood – for killing his friend. He would ultimately now annihilate the entire gang. They had crossed a line. It was total war. Yet, without Baruti, Rugova was at a loss how best to proceed. Someone would also need to deal with the Italians, should he be temporarily out of action. Payments and deliveries were due. Relationships needed to be maintained. Fears needed to be allayed, before the vultures started circulating. Hardened criminals were not the most forgiving of business associates, when things went awry. He couldn't afford to lose face with the Columbians, Hellbanianz and Turks too. The club would likely be shut down for an extended period. They would move less product, launder less money, as a result. Viktor oversaw half his operation, as well as being his eyes and ears. It would take ten trusted men to carry out just half his duties. After his lawyer, Rugova tried to get through to his accountant before the police reached his office. It was important to divert or hide his assets. Without money, he would be nothing. But the call went to voicemail.

Marshal didn't wait around to witness the raid on the nightclub. He drove home and, after a couple of large whiskies, fell asleep. When he woke, he checked various newsfeeds. There was no reference to eyewitnesses or CCTV footage of a suspect, in relation to the hit on three Albanian gangsters in the Canada Water area. The news report did mention that the murders were likely the result of a professional hit, carried out by a rival gang. Linked to the news report was an item on the arrest of Luka Rugova, an alleged senior figure in the Albanian mafia.

Job done.

23. Epilogue

Morning.

The world seemed a slightly more pleasant place, in the absence of Viktor Baruti. Marshal went for a run, although his body already felt like it was awash with endorphins from the start. The skies may have been grey, but his mood wasn't. A weight had somehow been lifted, like he was free from sin, since he killed again. He believed, for once, that he was running towards rather than away from something. It was like he was running downhill at the end – with the wind at his back – as he decided he would call Grace later in the day. He switched on the TV when back at the flat. No (new) news was good news. Some people can get away with murder. As a precaution he would dispose of the clothes he wore yesterday – and store the Glock at an alternative location. If, somehow, the police did knock on his door, he didn't want them to find any evidence.

He went to *Hej* before midday. Not only did Marshal drink a couple of coffees, both containing milk and two sugars, but he treated himself to a slice of apple pie too. Marshal smiled, as he thought of how he was more worried about Grace rejecting him than the police finding him a person of interest.

"How did the job with the fashion model go, by the way?" Jeremy Knight asked, after the two men came back into the coffee shop from smoking a cigarette.

"It wasn't quite what I was expecting. But that's a good thing. Grace was worth getting to know."

"It's unlike you to pay someone such a compliment."

"People can change."

"Are you back to being busy doing nothing?"

"We'll see."

The grey clouds dissipated, like wax burning away to reveal a painting underneath. Waves of sunlight lapped against Marshal's living room window, as he cradled a tumbler of brandy and lemonade, whilst listening to his – their – country music playlist.

"God blessed the broken road that led me straight to you."

A book lay open on the table next to him, but Marshal couldn't concentrate on the novel. Reality was proving too great a distraction. He rehearsed what he would say to Grace again, although he knew that life wasn't a movie or romantic comedy.

She may have the good sense to want nothing to do with me.

His phone chimed and Marshal's heart briefly swelled with hope, thinking that Grace had called.

"It seems you've been busy," Porter said, without any preamble. The fixer had watched the news. It took all his considerable reserves of English sangfroid to remain impassive, as Victoria sat next to him on the sofa, eating some strawberries and cream. He didn't know whether to be more shocked or impressed. The ex-Para had taken out both his enemies, in less than twenty-four hours. He briefly thought of the lost opportunity, in relation to Marshal declining to become one of his operatives years ago. He may have had a talent for the work – a calling. Like Devlin. Baruti was dead. Luka Rugova would not be seeing the light of day for some time. But as much as Marshal might have reminded the fixer of Michael Devlin, Porter didn't want him turning into his dead friend. "Is it all over now – mission accomplished?"

"Yes," Marshal replied.

Or I may just be getting started.

"I'm pleased to hear it. You've been able to pull your head out of the lion's mouth, James. You may not be so fortunate again. My offer stands, should you need a break and use of a holiday home. You don't have to travel alone, either. Victoria has asked me, or rather told me, to mention that Grace has been asking after you. My wife has mistaken me for a matchmaker, rather than a fixer, I warrant."

"I'll give Grace a call this afternoon. I promise."

Porter sat in his study and opened some post, after talking to Marshal. He received two party invites. The first was for an event in London, arranged by a think-tank called "The Fourth

Way". Lord Adonis was billed to give a speech, which madeup Porter's mind not to attend. Dante would have to create a new circle of Hell to house the cretins employed at the organisation. Or they could always be dismembered and distributed between the Fourth (Greed), Eighth (Fraud) and Ninth (Treachery) circles of Hell accordingly. He envisioned the gathering, filled with second-rate canapes and third-rate politicians. Special advisers and lobbyists would be scurrying around like death watch beetles, tapping on their phones and parroting the latest "progressive" views, which made them "relevant" to dim-witted millennials. He could hear the chorus of virtue-signalling about Brexit, as shrill as a soprano or dog whistle. Porter winced and sighed. He happily placed the invite in his wastepaper bin.

The second invitation was for a shooting party, hosted by Sir David Yarrow. Yarrow's father had been Porter's mentor and commanding officer in the Guards. Sir David Yarrow lived in elegant poverty, as he described it, on an estate close to Jeremy Corbyn's country pile on the Shropshire/Herefordshire border. His days were spent re-reading P. D. James novels ("I've read so many I think I'm beginning to look like her.") and courting his latest mistress, or mistresses. His wealth had largely contracted due to three expensive divorces. Each divorce had cost him a painting at the house – an Ansdell, Grimshaw and Jack Yeats respectively. His third wife had added insult to injury by marrying her divorce lawyer. The priapic sheep farmer got his revenge on his third wife by marrying her younger, prettier cousin. "Revenge is a dish best served cold, as cold as the frigid harpy," Yarrow had remarked to his old friend at the time. Porter read the letter, which accompanied the invite. "Rest assured I've banned senior civil servants, the French and any new money from attending the shoot… If you're unable to make it I might have to drink port late into the night with someone I despise or, worse, my wife." Porter checked his diary and decided to accept the invitation, partly because Victoria had just informed him that Henry Troughton had asked them over for dinner on the same day. The shoot furnished him with a genuine excuse to avoid his pompous neighbour. Porter would just make sure he packed a pair of cufflinks which were easy to remove and refasten, in case he needed to send a covert signal to his wife for them to leave the party.

Grace sat on a wooden bench, beneath a pear tree in the garden. Whether she knew it or not, she was wearing the same outfit she had worn when she first met Marshal. Her copy of *The End of the Affair* lay open on her lap, but she wasn't in the mood to read it. Violet sat on the bench next to her, either whimpering in sympathy with her pensive expression or, more likely, she wanted some attention – or a treat.

She had spent the morning dealing with some admin relating to the bookshop and speaking to the estate agent. She arranged a second viewing of the riverside property with Tamara. Grace thanked her for her help and said she would buy her lunch after the appointment, feeling guilty for the way she had treated her earlier in the week. Tamara asked if James would be joining them. "No."

The grass was cool on the soles of her bare feet, reminding her of when she had walked across the tiled floor towards Marshal's hotel room. Grace didn't quite know whether she should feel shame or regret about the incident. From the way she squirmed slightly on the bench, one would have thought she felt more shame, but should she never see Marshal again she knew she would feel more regret.

As she checked her phone to see if she had received a message from Marshal, his name flashed up on the screen. He was calling her. She smiled, took a breath and answered.

"Hello."

"Afternoon. How's your day?" Marshal asked, forgetting his lines already. Upon hearing her voice, he realised he missed it even more than he thought. The sound cut through his melancholy like an axe scything through the toughest timber.

Better for you being in it.

"I've mostly been dealing with estate agents. Your call is comfortably the highlight of my day. How have you been?"

"I've been fine. Sorry I wasn't in touch earlier. I've had a couple of things to take care of."

"Is everything okay?"

"Yes, it's a dead issue now."

Marshal smiled as he heard Violent whimper on the other end of the phone.

"Violet says hello. I think she misses you."

"She must be barking."

"I'm not sure whether she misses your bad puns, however."

"She's only human."

Grace laughed. The sound was intoxicating. Medicinal.

She was close to confessing that she missed him too.

"You may be wondering why I've called you," he added.

"Not so much. I'm just glad you have."

"I've lost the details to the launch party. I thought I might offer my meagre services as to how I can help with the event. We could meet when you're next in town, over lunch or dinner."

"I'll be free tomorrow night. My only condition is that you let me pay for dinner, as a thank you."

"Agreed. As a thank you for dinner though, you must let me take you to see the new production of Ivanov, which is on at The Old Vic."

As Marshal spoke, he also watched the muted TV. DI Martin Elwood was giving an interview on Sky News. The captions read how the police still didn't have any cast iron leads in relation to the "gangland killings" of the Albanians. But they had secured the arrest of the crime boss, Luka Rugova, and were confident of a conviction. "They sowed the seed, now they are going to reap the whirlwind," Elmwood remarked, quoting Arthur "Bomber" Harris. There may be hope for the police – and public – yet, Marshal considered.

"I'd enjoy that, thanks. Bugger, I've got the estate agents buzzing me. Is it okay if I talk to them? Otherwise, I may not be able to get through to them later.

"Of course. Would you like me to call you later?"

"No. I would *love* you to call me later."

After he hung up Marshal opened his laptop and booked a couple of tickets for the Chekhov play. He also confirmed his booking at the gun range.

End Note.

Enough is Enough is not an official sequel to *Gun For Hire*, but the books are complementary. Michael Devlin and James Marshal are similar, yet different.

The novels have been described as Catholic thrillers, black comedies and Graham Greene-like entertainments. "You might very well think that; I couldn't possibly comment," to quote a phrase.

One of the enjoyable aspects of writing contemporary, as opposed to historical, fiction is that I can include some people I know in the book – and the stories can have a soundtrack. As well as any music, I would encourage you to read any books recommended throughout the novels.

I would particularly like to thank Hej Coffee for their support. I would also understandably like to thank you, the reader. Should you have enjoyed *Enough Is Enough*, or *Gun For Hire*, please do email admin@sharpebooks.com and they will forward on any correspondence for me to reply to.

James Marshal and Oliver Porter will return in *Blood For Blood*.

Thomas Waugh.

*

Printed in Great Britain
by Amazon